THE UNSPEAKABLE GENTLEMAN

THE UNSPEAKABLE GENTLEMAN

JOHN P. MARQUAND

Originally published in 1922.

Published by Wildside Press for release in countries where it is in the public domain.

Visit us online at wildsidepress.com.

INTRODUCTION
KARL WURF

John Phillips Marquand (1893–1960) was a distinguished American novelist who carved a unique niche for himself in 20th-century literature. Born in Wilmington, Delaware, and raised in Rye, New York, and Newburyport, Massachusetts, Marquand's upbringing among the New England upper class provided a rich vein of material that he would mine throughout his career. After graduating from Harvard University, he worked as a journalist and served in World War I before turning to fiction, initially finding popular success with adventure and spy stories in magazines like *The Saturday Evening Post*.

Marquand's literary style was heavily influenced by the social realists of his time, most notably Sinclair Lewis. Like Lewis, Marquand possessed a keen eye for the subtle hypocrisies and rigid conventions governing the lives of the American elite. However, where Lewis often employed broad, biting satire, Marquand's approach was more nuanced and melancholic. He treated his subjects with a mixture of gentle irony and deep empathy, exploring the quiet desperation of individuals trapped by the expectations of their social class.

His enduring place in American letters was cemented by a series of critically acclaimed novels that satirized the Boston Brahmin society. His 1937 novel, *The Late George Apley*, earned him the Pulitzer Prize for Fiction and remains his most celebrated work. In it, and in subsequent novels like *Wickford Point* and *H.M. Pulham, Esquire*, Marquand masterfully used the flashback technique to reveal how the past perpetually shapes and constrains the present, a theme that became his signature.

Before achieving literary fame, Marquand was also a master of genre fiction, particularly in the mystery and espionage fields. His most famous creation was the astute and unfailingly polite Japanese secret agent, Mr. I. O. Moto. The Mr. Moto series, which includes titles such as *Your Turn, Mr. Moto* and *Think Fast, Mr. Moto*, were thrilling, fast-paced tales of international intrigue that captivated readers and were adapted into a popular series of films. These stories demonstrated his versatility and skill in crafting suspenseful, engaging plots.

Although *The Unspeakable Gentleman* showcases his early talent for historical adventure, readers who enjoy his sharp characterizations and exploration of social mores will find much to admire in his other works. His Pulitzer Prize-winning novel, *The Late George Apley*, offers a definitive and subtly humorous portrait of a Boston blue blood. For a compelling look at the pressures of conformity, *H.M. Pulham, Esquire* is an excellent choice.

Marquand's ability to blend popular storytelling with serious social commentary makes his work as relevant today as it was in his time. He explored timeless themes of identity, regret, and the struggle for individual freedom against the backdrop of a rapidly changing America, securing his legacy as a masterful chronicler of the human condition.

CHAPTER I

I HAVE SEEN THE improbable turn true too often not to have it disturb me. Suppose these memoirs still exist when the French royalist plot of 1805 and my father's peculiar role in it are forgotten. I cannot help but remember it is a restless land across the water. But surely people will continue to recollect. Surely these few pages, written with the sole purpose of explaining my father's part in the affair, will not degenerate into anything so pitifully fanciful as the story of a man who tried his best to be a bad example because he could not be a good one.

It was my Uncle Jason who was with me when I learned of my father's return to America. I still remember the look of sympathetic concern on his broad, good-natured face, as I read my father's letter. There was anxiety written there as he watched me, for my uncle was a kindly, thoughtful man. For the moment he seemed to have quite forgotten the affairs of his counting house, and the inventory of goods from France, which a clerk had placed before him. Of late he had taken in me an unaccustomed interest, in no wise allayed by the letter I was holding.

"So he is here," said my Uncle Jason.

"He is just arrived," I answered.

"I had heard of it," he remarked thoughtfully. "And you will see him, Henry?"

"Yes," I replied, "since she asked me to."

"She had asked you? Your mother? You did not tell me that." His voice had been sharp and reproachful, and then he had sighed. "After all," he went on more gently, "he is your father, and you must respect him as such, Henry, hard as it is to do so. I am sorry, almost, that he and I have quarreled, for in many ways your father was a remarkable man who might have gone far, except for his failing. God knows I did my best to help him."

And he sighed again at the small success of his efforts and returned to the papers that lay before him on the counting house table. His business had become engrossing of late, and gave him little leisure.

"Do not be too hard on him, Henry," he said, as I departed.

It was ten years since I had seen my father, ten years when we change more than we do during the rest of a lifetime. Ten years back we had lived in a great house with lawns that ran down to the river where our ships pulled at their moorings. My father and I had left the house together—I for school, and my father—I have never learned where he had gone. I was just beginning to see the starker outlines of a world that has shaken off the shadows of youth when I saw him again.

I remember it was a morning early in autumn. The wind was fresh off the sea, making the pounding of the surf on the beach seem very near as I urged my horse from the neat, quiet streets of the town up the rutted lane that led to the Shelton house. The tang of the salt marshes was in the wind, and a touch of frost over the meadows told me the ducks would soon be coming in from shelter. Already the leaves were falling off the tall elms, twisting in little spirals through the clear October sunlight.

And yet, in spite of the wind and the sea and the clean light of the forenoon, there was a sadness about the place, and an undercurrent of uneasy silence that the rustling of the leaves and the noise of the surf only seemed to accentuate. It was like the silence that falls about a table when the guests have left it, and the chairs are empty and the lights are growing dim. It was the silence that comes over all places where there should be people, and yet where no one comes.

The shrubbery my grandfather had brought from England was more wild and disordered than when I had seen it last. The weeds had choked the formal garden that once grew before the front door. And the house—I had often pictured that house in my memory—with its great arched doorway, its small-paned windows and its gambrel roof. Once it had seemed to me a massive and majestic structure. Now those ten years had made it shrink to a lonely, crumbling building that overlooked the harbor mouth. Clematis had swarmed over the bricks, a tangle of dead and living vines. The paint was chipping from the doors and window ledges. Here and there a shutter had broken loose and was sagging on rusted hinges. Houses are apt to follow the direction their owners take.

I knew I was being watched, though I cannot tell how I knew it. Yet I saw nothing until I was nearly at our door. I remember I was noticing the green stain from the brass knocker on its paneling, when my horse snorted and stopped dead in his tracks. From the overgrown clump of lilacs that flanked the granite stone which served as a door-step something was glinting in the sun, and then as I looked more closely, I saw a face peering at me from between the twigs, a face of light mahogany with thick lips that showed the presence of negro blood. It was Brutus, my father's half-caste servant.

Dark and saturnine as ever, he glided out into the path in front of me, thrusting something back into the sash around his waist, moved toward me, and took my horse's head. His teeth shone when I spoke to him, but he said never a word in return to my greeting. There was a touch of Indian in his blood that made his speech short and laconic. Nevertheless, he was glad to see me. He grasped my shoulder as I dismounted, and shook me gently from side to side. His great form loomed before me, his lips framed in a cheerful grin, his eyes appraising and friendly. And then I noticed for the first time the livid welt of a cut across his cheek. Brutus read my glance, but he only shook his head in answer.

"What do you mean, hiding in those bushes?" I asked him roughly.

"Always must see who is coming," said Brutus. "Monsieur may not want to see who is coming—you understan'?"

"No," I said, "I don't understand."

His grasp on my shoulder tightened.

"Then you go home," he said, "You go home now. Something happen. Monsieur very angry. Something bad—you understan'?"

"He is in the house?" I asked.

Brutus nodded.

"Then take this horse," I said, and swung open the front door.

A draft eddied through the broad old hallway as I stepped over the threshold, and there was a smell of wood smoke that told me the chimneys were still cold from disuse. Someone had stored the hall full of coils of rope and sailcloth, but in the midst of it the same tall clock was ticking out its cycle, and the portraits of the Shelton family still hung against the white panels.

The long, brown rows of books still lined the walls of the morning room. The long mahogany table in the center was still littered with maps and papers. There were the same rusted muskets and small swords in the rack by the fireplace, and in front of the fire in a great, high-backed armchair my father was sitting. I paused with a curious feeling of doubt, surprise and diffidence. Somehow I had pictured a different meeting and a different man. He must surely have heard my step and the jingling of my spurs as I crossed the room, but he never so much as raised his head. He still rested, leaning indolently back, watching the flames dance up the chimney. He was dressed in gray satin small clothes that went well with his slender figure. His wig was fresh powdered, and his throat and wrists were framed in spotless lace. The care of his person was almost the only tribute he paid to his past.

I must have stood for twenty seconds watching him while he watched the fire, before he turned and faced me, and when he did I had forgotten the words I had framed to greet him. I knew he was preparing to meet a hard ordeal. He knew as well as I there was no reason why I should be glad to see him. Yet he showed never a trace of uncertainty. His eye never wavered. His lips were drawn in the same supercilious upward curve that gave him the expression I most often remembered. Ten years had not done much to change him. The pallor I had remembered on his features had been burned off by a tropical sun. That was all. There was hardly a wrinkle about his eyes, hardly a tell-tale crease in his high forehead. Wherever he had been, whatever he had done, his serenity was still unshaken. It still lay over him, placid and impenetrable. And when he spoke, his voice was cool and impassive and cast in pleasant modulation.

"So you are here," he remarked, as though he were weighing each word carefully, "and why did you come? I think I told you in my letter there was no need unless you wished."

There was something cold and unfriendly in his speech. I tried in vain to fight down a rising feeling of antagonism, a vague sense of disappointment. For a moment we glanced at each other coldly.

"I think, sir," I answered, "from a sense of curiosity."

Almost as soon as I had spoken, I was sorry, for some sixth sense told me I had hurt him. With a lithe, effortless grace he rose from his chair and faced me, and his smile, half amused, half tolerant, curved his lips again.

"I should have known you would be frank," he said, "Your letter, my son, refusing to accept my remittances, should have taught me as much, but we grow forgetful as our feet weary of the path of life."

Yet I remember thinking that few people looked less weary than my father as he stood there watching me. The primroses, it seemed, had afforded pleasant footing.

I believe he read my thoughts, for it seemed to me that for an instant genuine amusement was written in his glance, but there were few genuine emotions he allowed free play.

"Perhaps," he suggested pleasantly, "it would interest you to know why I have returned to these rather rigorous and uncongenial surroundings. If not, I beg you to be frank again, Henry. There's nothing that I dread more than being stupid."

"Sir," I objected, "I told you I was curious."

"To be sure you did," he admitted. "Can it be possible that I am becoming absent-minded? Henry, I am going to tell you something very flattering. Can you believe it? It is largely on your account that I consented to revisit these familiar scenes!"

"No," I said, "I cannot, sir, since you ask me."

My father shrugged his shoulders. "Far be it from me to overstrain your credulity, my son," he observed blandly. "Let us admit then there was also some slight factor of expedience—but slight, Henry, almost negligible, in fact. It happened that I was in a French port, and that while there I should think of you."

"Sir," I said, "You startle me!"

But he continued, regardless of my interruption.

"And what should be there also, but the *Eclipse*, ready to set for home! Quite suddenly I determined to sail her back. I, too, was curious, my son." For a moment his voice lost its bantering note. "Curious," he continued gravely, "to know whether you were a man like me, or one of whom I might have reason to be proud.... So here we are, Henry. Who said coincidence was the exception and not the rule?"

His last words drifted gently away, and in their wake followed an awkward silence. The logs were hissing in the fire. I could hear the clock in the hall outside, and the beating of the vines against the window panes. It was no sound, certainly, that made me whirl around to look behind me,—some instinct—that was all. There was Brutus, not two feet from my back, with my father's cloak over his right arm, and my father's sword held in his great fist.

"Do not disturb yourself, Brutus," said my father. "We are both gentlemen, more or less, and will not come to blows. My cloak, Brutus. I am sorry, my son, that we must wait till later in the day to exchange ideas. Even here in America affairs seem to follow me. Will you content yourself till evening? There are horses in the stable and liquors in the cellar. Choose all or either, Henry. Personally, I find them both amusing."

He stood motionless, however, even when his dark cloak was adjusted to his shoulders, as though some matters were disturbing him; and then he tapped his sword hilt with a precise, even motion of his fingers.

"Brutus," he said slowly, "I shall take my pistols also."

"Your pistols!" I echoed. "You have forgotten you are back in America."

He half turned toward me, and favored me with a serene, incurious glance. "On the contrary," he said, "I am just beginning to remember."

And so without further words he left me. I followed him through our rear doorway, out over the crumbling bricks of our terrace, which had been built to overlook the river, and watched him walk slowly and thoughtfully down the path with its border of elm trees, to his warehouses, where a half dozen men had already started work.

The river was dark blue under a cloudless sky. The sunlight was playing in restless sparkles where the wind ruffled the water's surface. Out near the channel I could see the *Eclipse* riding at anchor, her decks littered with bales and gear, and the *Sun Maid* and the *Sea Tern*, trim and neat, and down deep in the water as though ready to put to sea. At the head of our wharf were bales and boxes stacked in the odd confusion that comes of a hasty discharge of cargo.

On the terrace where I was standing I could see the other wharves along the waterfront, and the church spires and roofs of the town reared among the trees that lined the busy streets. Toward the sand dunes the marshes stretched away in russet gold into the autumn haze. The woods across the river were bright patches of reds and yellows, pleasant and inviting in the sunlight.

But I saw it all with only half an eye. I was still thinking of the dark hall behind me, and the cold, unwelcome stillness of the shuttered rooms. I could understand his depression, now that he had come back to it. But there was something else.... I was still thinking of it when I looked at the *Eclipse* again. It would have been hard to find a craft of more delicate, graceful lines. They often said he had a flair for ships and women. A shifting current, some freak of the wind and tide, was making her twist and pull at her anchor, and for a moment the sun struck clean on her broadside. A gaping hole between decks had connected two of her ports in a jagged rent.

It was not surprising. My father's ships were often fired on at sea. Nor was it strange that Brutus had a half-healed scar on his cheek. But why had my father gone armed to his own wharf? Perhaps I might have forgotten if I had not visited the stables.

Our carriage harness still hung from the pegs, dried and twisted by the years, and minus its silver trimmings. The sunlight filtered through cracks in the roof, and danced through the dust mites to the rows of vacant stalls. Near the door my horse was feeding comfortably, and beside him stood two bays that shone from careful grooming. One was carrying a saddle with a pair of pistols in the pocket. Yet not a hair had been turned from riding.

CHAPTER II

I RODE THROUGH TOWN that afternoon, and it was not entirely because time hung heavily on my hands. We were proud of our town. The houses were as elegant and substantial as any you could find. Our streets were broad and even. Our walks were paved with brick. There was not a finer tavern than ours to the north of Boston, or better dressed men frequenting it. Men said in those days that we would be a great seaport; that the world would look more and more to that northern Massachusetts river mouth. They had spoken thus of many other harbor towns in the centuries that men have gone down to the sea. I think they have been wrong almost as often as they had predicted. The ships have ceased to sail over the bar. No one heeds the rotting planking of the wharves. The clang of hammers and the sailors' songs have gone, and trade and gain and venture have gone with them.

Strange, as I recall that afternoon. They were building a new L to the tavern. Tradespeople were busy about their shops. Coaches newly painted, and drawn by well-matched horses, rolled by me. Gentlemen in bright new coats, servants in new family livery, sailors from the docks, clerks from the counting houses, all gave the street a busy air—lent it a pleasant assurance of affluence.

I was mistaken when I thought I could ride by as a stranger might. It seemed to me that there was no one too busy to stop and look, to turn and whisper a word to someone else. They had learned already that I was my father's son. I could feel a hot flame of anger burning my cheeks, the old, stinging passion of resentment I had felt so often when my father's name was mentioned. They knew me. Their looks alone told that, but never a nod, or smile of greeting, marked my return.

Though I had never spoken to them, I knew them all—the Penfields, father and son, tall and lean with bony faces and sandy hair and eyebrows, and restless, pale blue eyes—Squire Land, small and ascetic, his lips constantly puckered as though he had tasted something unpleasant. Captain Proctor, stouter than when I had seen him last, with the benign good nature that comes of settled affairs and good living. Over them and over the town, those eight years had passed with a light hand.

But it was not our town I had come to visit. I found Ned Aiken, as I knew I should, with the *Eclipse* in harbor. He was seated on his door step by the river road, as though he had always been planted in that very place. I remember expecting he would be glad to see me. Instead, he took his pipe from his mouth, and gazed at me steadily, like some steer stopped from grazing. Then he placed his pipe on the stone step, and rose slowly to his feet, squat and burly, his little eyes glinting below his greasy, unbraided hair, his jaw protruding and ominous. Slowly he loosened the dirty red handkerchief he kept swathed about his throat, and raised a stubby hand to push the hair from his heavy forehead. Then his face relaxed into a grim smile, and he seated himself on the step again.

"You've changed since last I saw you," he said; "changed remarkable, you have. Why, right now I thought you might be someone else."

Had Brutus also been laboring under the same delusion?

I told him I was glad we were still on speaking terms, and seated myself beside him. He studied me for a while in silence, leisurely puffing at his pipe.

"You mistook me for someone?" I asked finally.

"Yes," said Mr. Aiken, and slapped his pipe against the palm of his hand. "You've been shootin' up, you have, since I set eyes on you."

He paused, seemingly struck by a genial inspiration.

"Yes, shootin' up." Still looking at me he gave way to a hoarse chuckle.

"Why, boy, we've all been doing some shootin'—you, your dad, and me too—since we seen you last," and he was taken by a paroxysm of silent mirth.

"Now that's what I call wit!" he gasped complacently, and then he repeated in joyous encore:

"You shootin'—me shootin'—he shootin'."

"You weren't shooting at anybody?" I asked with casual innocence.

"And why shouldn't we be, I want to know?" he demanded, but his tongue showed no sign of slipping. His glance had resumed its old stolid watchfulness, which caused me to remain tactfully silent.

"But we wasn't shootin' at anybody," Mr. Aiken concluded, more genially. "Not at anybody, just at selected folks."

He stopped to glance serenely about him, and somehow the dusty road, the river, the trees and the soft sunlight seemed to make him strangely confiding. His harsh voice lowered in gentle patronage.

"Would you like to know who those folks were?" he asked finally.

I must have been too eager in giving my assent, for Mr. Aiken smiled broadly and nodded his head with complacent satisfaction.

"I thought you would admire to," said Mr. Aiken; "like as not you'd give a tooth to know, now wouldn't you? Never do know a tooth is useful till you lose it. Now look at me—I've had as many as six stove out off an' on, and now—But you wanted to know who it was we shot at, didn't you? So you did, boy, so you did. Well, I'll tell you, so I will. Yes, so help me if I don't tell you, boy." And his voice trailed off in a low chuckle.

"It was folks like you," he concluded crisply; "folks who didn't mind their own business."

Gleefully he repeated the sentence. Its ringing cadence and the trend of his whole discourse gave him evident pleasure, and even caused him to continue further with his rebuke.

"There you have it," said Mr. Aiken, "the Captain's own words, b'Gad. 'Mr. Aiken', he says, 'I fancy we may meet a number of people whose affairs will not stop them interfering with our own. If you see any,' he says, 'shoot them, Mr. Aiken'."

He had lapsed into a good-natured, reminiscent mood, and, as he fixed his gaze on the trees across the road, he was prompted to enlarge still further on the episode. He seemed to have forgotten I was there as he continued.

"I wish it had been on deck," he remarked, "instead of a place with damned gold chairs and gold on the ceiling, and cloth on the walls, and velvets such as respectable folks use for dress and not for ornament, and candles in gold sticks, and the floor like a sheet of ice.

"Hell," said Mr. Aiken. "I'd sooner slip on blood than on a floor like that. Yes, so I would. I wonder why those frog eaters don't make their houses snug and decent instead of big as a church. Now, though I'm not a moral man, yet I call it immoral, damned if I don't, to live in a house like that."

"Yet somehow pleasant," I ventured politely, "surely you have found that the beauty of most immoral things. They all seem to be pleasant. Am I not right, Mr. Aiken?"

He looked at me sharply, shrugged his shoulders, and denied me the pleasure of an answer.

"Not that I meant to puzzle you," I added hastily, "but you have sailed so long with my father, that I considered you in a position to know. Now in France—"

Mr. Aiken dropped his pipe.

"Who said anything about France?" he demanded.

"And did you not?" I asked, beginning to enjoy my visit. "Surely you were speaking just now about a chateau, the scene of some pleasant adventure. Pray don't let me interrupt you."

A bead of perspiration rolled down Mr. Aiken's brow, and he tightened his handkerchief about his throat, as though to stifle further conversation. He sat silent for a minute while his mind seemed to wander off into a maze of dim recollections, and his eyes half-closed, the better to see the pictures that drifted through his memory.

"What am I here ashore and sober for," he asked finally, "so I won't talk, that's why, and I won't talk, so there's the end of it. It's just that I have to have my little joke, that's all, or I wouldn't have said anything about the chato or the Captain either.

"Though, if I do say it," he added in final justification, "there ain't many seafaring men who have a chance to sail along of a man like him."

"And how does that happen?" I asked.

"Because there ain't any more like him to sail with."

He sat watching me, and the gap between us seemed to widen. He seemed to be looking at me from some great distance, from the end of the road where years and experience had led him, full of thoughts he could never express, even if the desire impelled him.

"No, not any," said Mr. Aiken.

The dusk was beginning to gather when I rode home, the heavy purple dusk of autumn, full of the crisp smell of dead leaves and the low hanging wood smoke from the chimneys.

My father was reading Voltaire beside a briskly burning fire. Closing his book on his forefinger, he waved me to a chair beside him.

"My son," he said, "they mix better than you think, Voltaire and gunpowder. Have you not found it so?"

"I fear," I replied, "that my experience has been too limited. Give me time, sir, I have only been twice to sea. Next time I shall remember to take Voltaire with me."

"Do," he advised courteously; "you will find it will help with the privateers—tide you over every little unpleasantness. Ah yes, it is advice worth following. I learned it long ago—a little difference of opinion—and the pages of the great philosopher—"

He raised his arm and glanced at it critically.

"Words well placed—is it not wonderful, their steadying effect—the deadly accuracy which their logic seems to impart to the hand and eye? A man can be dangerous indeed with twenty pages of Voltaire behind him."

He took a pinch of snuff, and leaned forward to tap me gently on the knee, his expression coldly genial.

"I have read all the works of Voltaire, Henry, read them many times."

Unbidden, a picture of him came before me in a room with gilt chairs and candelabra whose glass pendants sparkled in the mild yellow light—with a smell of powder mingling strangely with the scent of flowers.

"But why," he concluded, "should I be more explicit than Mr. Aiken? To fear nothing, say nothing. It is a maxim followed by so many politicians. Strange that it still stays valuable. Strange—"

And he waved his hand in a negligent gesture of deprecation.

"Why, indeed, be more explicit," I rejoined. "Your sudden interest is quite enough to leave me overcome, sir, when, after years of neglect, you see to it I ride out safely of an afternoon."

He tapped his snuff box thoughtfully.

"Coincidence again, Henry, that is all. How was I to know you would be outside Ned Aiken's house while I was within?"

"And how should I know that paternal care would prompt you to remain within while I was without?"

For a second it seemed to me that my father was going to laugh—for a fraction of a second something like astonishment seemed to take possession of him. Then Brutus appeared in the doorway.

"My son," he said, as I followed him to supper, "I must compliment you. Positively you improve upon acquaintance."

CHAPTER III

I HAD REMEMBERED HIM as a man who disliked talk. I had often seen him sit for hours on end without a word, looking at nothing in particular, with his expressionless serenity. But on this particular evening the day's activities appeared to have made his social instincts vividly assertive, and to arouse him to unusual, and almost unnatural animation. As we sat at a small round table beside the dining room fireplace, he launched into a cheerful discourse, ignoring completely any displeasure I attempted to assume. The great room with its dingy wainscot only half lighted by the candles on the table before us, was cluttered with a hundred odds and ends that collect in a deserted house—a ladder, a stiff, rusted bridle, a coil of frayed rope, a kettle, a dozen sheets of the Gazette, empty bottles, dusty crockery and broken chairs. He surveyed them all with a bland, uncritical glance. From his manner he might have been surrounded by brilliant company. From his conversation he might have been in a pot house.

I noticed at once what many had been at pains to mention to me before—that my father was not a temperate man. Nor did our cellar seem wholly bleak. He pressed wine upon me, and soon had finished a bottle himself, only to gesture Brutus to uncork a second. And all the while he regaled me with anecdotes of the gaming table and the vices of a dozen seaports. With hardly a pause he described a lurid succession of drinking bouts and gallant adventures. He finished a second bottle of wine, and was half way through a third. Yet all the while his voice never lost its pleasant modulation. Never a flush or an increase of animation came to change him. Politely detached, he discoursed of love and murder, gambling and chicanery, drawing on the seemingly exhaustless background of his own experience for illustration. He seemed to have known the worst men from all the ends of the earth, to have shared in their business and their pleasures. He seemed to have been in every discreditable undertaking that came beneath his notice. In retrospect they pleased him—all and every one.

What he saw when he glanced at me appeared to please him also. At any rate, it gave him the encouragement that one usually receives from an attentive listener.

"Brutus, again a bottle. It is at the fourth bottle," he explained, "that I am at my best. It is the fourth bottle, or perhaps the fifth, that seems to free me from the restraints that old habits and early education have wound about me. *In vino veritas*, my son, but the truth must be measured in quarts for each individual. Some men I know might be drowned in wine and still be hypocrites, so solidly are their heads placed upon their shoulders. But my demands are modest, my son, just as modest as I am a modest sinner."

He called to Brutus to toss more wood upon the fire, leaned back for a while, holding his glass to the light of the flames, and turned to me again with his cool, perfunctory smile.

"Strange, is it not, that men through all the ages have sought fools and charlatans to tell their fortunes, when a little wine is clearer than the most mystic ball of crystal. Before the bottle the priests of Egypt and the Delphic oracle seem as faint, my son, as the echoes in a snail shell. Palmistry and astrology—let us fling them into the whirlpool of vanity! But give a man wine enough, and any observer can tell his possibilities. A touch of it—and where are the barriers with which he has surrounded himself? Another drop, and how futile are all the deceptions which he is wont to practice upon others! In St. Kitts once I drank wine with a most respectable merchant, a man who carried the Bible beside his snuff box, and referred to both almost as frequently as he did to the profit and balance on his ledger. And would you believe it? The next time he met me, he blamed me for the loss of many thousands of pounds. He even laid at my door certain reprehensible indiscretions of his wife, though I could have told him that night over the glasses that both were inevitable long before either occurred.

"But pray do not look at me so blankly, my son. It was not clairvoyance on my part—merely simple reasoning, aided by very excellent and very heady Madeira. How true it is that there is truth in wine—and money too, if the grape is used to the proper advantage.

"Again—some men talk of fortune at cards, good luck or bad, but as for me, I can tell how the luck will run by the number of bottles that are placed beside the table. A little judgment, and the crudest reasoning—that is all. But doubtless mutual friends have already hinted to you of my propensities at cards—and other things. Is it not so, my son?"

Was it the gentle inflection of the question, or his intent glance that made me feel, as I had felt before that day, that I was face to face with an alert antagonist? He called on me to speak, and I was loth to break my silence. If he had only left me to my own bitter thoughts,—but why should I have expected him to be tactful? Why should I have expected him to be different from the gossip that clouded his name?

"Your card playing is still remembered, sir," I told him. "I have heard of it two months back."

Deliberately he pushed one of the candles aside, so that the light should stand less between us, poured himself another glass of wine, and flicked the dust from the bottle off his sleeve.

"Indeed?" was his comment. "Your memory does you credit, even though youthful impressions are apt to lodge fast. Or shall I say it is only another proof of the veracity of my man of business? Two months ago, at a certain little gathering, someone, whose name I have yet to discover, informed you of certain bad habits I had contracted in games of chance. I remember being interested at the time that my reputation lasted so well in my absence. But I beg you—let me confirm the report still further. Am I mistaken in believing you made some apt retort?"

"Sir," I said in a voice that sounded strangely discordant, "I told him he lied."

"Ha!" said my father, and for a moment I thought he was going to commend my act, but instead his eyes moved to the table.

"Brutus," he continued, "is my mind becoming cloudy, or is it true the wine is running low? Open another bottle, Brutus."

There was a silence while he raised his glass to his lips.

"And am I right," he asked, "in recalling that you allowed yourself the liberty—of punctuating that comment?"

"You have been well informed, sir," I answered. "I struck him in the face."

He waved a hand to me in a pleasant gesture of acknowledgment, and half turned in his chair, the better to speak over his shoulder.

"Did I hear aright, Brutus?" he inquired. "There's faith for you and loyalty! He called the boy a liar who called me a cheat at cards! Ah, those illusions of youth! Ah for that sweet mirage that used to glitter in the sky overhead! It's only the wine that brings it back today—called him a liar, Brutus, and gave him the blow!"

"But pardon," he went on. His voice was still grave and slow, though his lips were bent in a bitter little smile. His face had reddened, and it was the wine, I think, that made his eyes dance in the candle light. "Overlook, I beg, the rudeness of my interruption. The exceptional in your narrative quite intrigues me, my son. Doubtless your impulsive action led to the conventional result?"

There he sat, amusedly examining me, smiling at my rising temper. My reply shaped itself almost without my volition.

"Excuse me, sir," I retorted, "if I say the result was more natural than your action upon a greater provocation."

"Had it ever occurred to you, my son, that perhaps my self-control was greater also? Let us call it so, at any rate, and go on with our adventure."

"As you will, sir," I said. "We all make our mistakes."

He raised his eyebrows in polite surprise, and his hand in a gesture of protest.

"Our mistakes? Was I not right in believing you had a competent instructor? I begin to fear your education is deficient. Surely you have agility and courage. Why a mistake, my son?"

"The mistake," I replied, "was in the beginning and not in the end. I made the error in believing he told an untruth."

"Indeed?" said my father. "Thank you, Brutus, I have had wine enough for the evening. Do you not consider your error—how shall we put it—quite inexcusable in view of the other things you have doubtless heard?"

But I could only stare dumbly at him across the table.

"Come, come," he continued. "How goes the gossip now? Surely there is more about me. Surely you have heard"—he paused to drain the dregs in his glass—"the rest?"

I eyed him for a moment in silence before I answered, but he met my glance fairly, indulging apparently in the same curiosity, half idle, half cynical, that he might have displayed before some episode of the theatre. It was a useless question that he asked. He knew too well that the answer was obvious.

"Yes," I said, "I have heard it."

"So," he exclaimed cheerfully, "my reputation still continues. Wonderful, is it not, how durable a bad reputation is, and how fragile a good one. One bounds back like a rubber ball. The other shatters like a lustre punch bowl. And did the same young man—I presume he was young—enlighten you about this, the most fatal parental weakness?"

"No," I said, "I learned of it later."

He raised his hand and began gently stroking his coat lapel, his fingers quickly crossing it in a vain search for some imaginary wrinkle, moving back and forth with a steady persistence, while he watched me, still amused, still indifferent.

"And might I ask who told you?" he inquired.

"Your brother-in-law," I replied, "My Uncle Jason."

"Dieu!" cried my father, "but I grow careless."

He was looking ruefully at his lapel. Somehow the threads had given way, and there was a rent in the gray satin.

"Another coat ruined," he observed, and the raillery was gone from his voice. "How fortunate it is that the evening is well along, and bed time is nearly here. One coat torn in the brambles, and one with a knife, and now—But your uncle was right, quite right in telling you. Indeed, I should have done the same myself. The truth first, my son. Always remember that."

And he turned again to his coat.

"I told him I did not believe it," I ventured, but the appeal in my voice, if there was any, passed him quite unnoticed.

"Indeed?" he said. "Brutus, you will put an extra blanket on my bed, for I fancy the night air is biting."

I pushed back my chair.

"And now, you will excuse me" I said, "if I take my leave."

I rose a trifle unsteadily, and stood before him, with no particular effort to hide my anger and contempt. But apparently I had ceased to be of interest. He was sitting just as I had first seen him that morning, staring into the embers of the fire. As I watched him, even through my anger I felt a vague regret, a touch of pity—pity for a life that was wasted in spite of its possibilities, in boasting and blackguardry. I began hoping that he would speak, would argue or remonstrate. Instead, he said nothing, only sat serenely indifferent, his eyes still on the fire. Stepping around the debris that filled the room, I had placed my hand on the latch, when I heard a stealthy footstep behind me. Brutus was at my elbow. There was a tinkle of a wine glass falling on the hearth. I turned to see my father facing me beside the table I had quitted—the calm modulation gone from his voice, his whole body poised and alert, as though ready to spring through the space that separated us.

"No doubt," he said, drawing a deep breath, "you are leaving this house because you cannot bear to stay under the same roof with a man of my stamp and accomplishments. Come, is that the reason?"

"Only partly," I answered, turning to face him, and then the words tripped off my tongue, hot and bitter, before I had wit to check them. "What right have I to be particular, now that I have found out my inheritance? Why should I pick my company? Why should I presume to hold my head up? I can only be blessed now, sir, like the rest of the meek."

I paused to let my final words sink in, and because I knew they would hurt him, I spoke them with an added satisfaction.

"I shall start at once to acquire merit which the moth cannot corrupt," I continued. "I am leaving to apologize to the man I fought with because he called you a cheat—and to my uncle for doubting his word."

My father's fist came down on the table with a crash.

"Then, by God," he shouted, "you'll not leave this room! You'll not take a single step until you've learned two things, learned them so you'll never forget. Stand where you are and listen!"

CHAPTER IV

I REMEMBER THE CURIOUS feeling I had that my father was gone, that he had vanished while my back was turned, leaving me to face someone else. Then, as I stared at him, still unready and speechless, the light died out of his eyes, his lips relaxed, and his hand went up to arrange the lace at his throat.

"Shun my example," he said, "shudder at the life I have led. Call me dissolute. Call me dangerous company. Say that in every way I'm unfit to be your father—say that I'm an outcast, suitable only as material for slander. I will agree with you. I will teach you that your judgment is correct. Let us only set two limits and do not call them virtues. They are necessities in the life I lead, nothing more. They—"

The sound at the knocker on the front door broke into my father's speech and stilled it. In the pause, while the echoes died away, he shrugged his shoulders negligently, and settled himself back in his chair.

"My son," he sighed, "allow me to point out the misfortune of being a man of affairs. They will never adjust themselves to the proper time and place. Brutus, the two gentlemen about whom I was speaking—show them in at once. And you, my son, there is no need for you to leave. The evening is young yet."

"Where are you, Shelton?" came a sharp, authoritative voice from the hallway. "Damn this dark passage."

"Open the door, Henry," my father said.

As I did so, two gentlemen entered. The taller, without bothering to remove his hat, strode over to my father's chair. The other stood undecided near the threshold, until Brutus closed the door behind him. Without rising from his chair, my father gave first one and then the other, the impartial, casual glance of the disinterested observer.

"This," he remarked politely, "comes near to being unexpected. I had heard you had come to town, but I had hoped to meet you only in some desolate waste of purgatory. I fear your visitation finds me singularly unprepared to do the duties of a host. You found the passage dark? Ah, Lawton, I fear it will be darker still where you are going."

"That's enough, Shelton," interrupted the first gentleman. "I didn't come here to hear you talk. I've heard you do that often enough in the old days. You can talk a woman off her feet, but by God, you can't talk me."

My father waved his hand negligently, as though disavowing some compliment.

"The same forceful character," he observed gently, "the same blunt candor. How refreshing it is, Lawton, after years of intrigue and dissimulation. My son, this is Mr. Lawton, an old, but he will pardon me if I do not add—a valued acquaintance."

For a moment Mr. Lawton's pale eyes looked sharply into mine, and I bowed to him ironically. I saw a high, thin face, resolute and impulsive, a grim ascetic face, with a long, straight nose that seemed pulled too close to his upper lip, and a mouth stamped roughly on a narrow, bony jaw, a mouth, as I looked at it, that seemed ready to utter an imprecation.

"Mr. Lawton and I have met before," I said.

"Indeed? And our friend in the background," my father continued. "Perhaps it is my bad memory that permits his identity still to be a revelation?"

The stranger nervously arranged a fold in his sea cloak, while his little black eyes darted restlessly about the room.

"It's Sims, Captain Shelton," he volunteered, in a gentle, unassuming voice, "and very much at your service."

"Captain Shelton be damned!" snapped Lawton. "Keep your name to yourself, Sims, and watch the negro and the boy. Now, Shelton, for the reason why I'm here."

"Indeed, I am forced to admit the reason for your visit may have its pertinence," my father admitted. "The fatigues of a long day, coupled with the evening's wine—" He stifled a yawn behind the back of his hand, and smiled in polite deprecation.

Slight as was his speech, Mr. Lawton seemed to take a deep interest in it. Indeed, even while he backed around the table and seated himself in the chair I had occupied, my father's slightest expression engaged his undivided attention. There fell a silence such as sometimes comes at a game of cards when the stakes at the table are running higher than is pleasant. Brutus was watching Mr. Sims with a malignant intensity. Mr. Sims watched Brutus. Mr. Lawton's eyes, as I have said, never left my father, and my father polished his nails on the sleeve of his coat.

"Did I understand you to say," he asked finally, "that you were planning to relieve my mind of the burden of speculation?"

"Quite," said Mr. Lawton, with a poor attempt at dryness. "I have come here tonight to induce or force you to return a piece of stolen property. I give you the liberty of taking your choice. Either—"

His voice raised itself to a sharp command.

"*Damn you, Shelton, sit still!*"

The picture had changed. Mr. Lawton was leaning across the table, levelling a pistol at my father's head. With a detached, academic interest, my father glanced at the weapon, and, without perceptible pause, without added haste or deliberation, he continued to withdraw the hand he had thrust into his right coat pocket. Beside me I heard Brutus draw a sharp breath. I saw Mr. Sims fumble under his cloak and take a quick step backwards. There was a tense, pregnant silence, broken by Mr. Sims in fervent expletive. My father had withdrawn his hand. He was holding in it his silver snuff box, which he tossed carelessly on the table, where it slid among the wine bottles.

"Why strain so at a gnat, Lawton," he continued in his old conversational manner. "Though one can kill a sparrow with a five pound shot, is it worth the effort? Small as my personal regard is for you, a note penned in three lines would have brought you back your trinket. But when you say it is stolen—"

With a gesture of exasperation, Mr. Lawton attempted to interrupt.

"When you say it is stolen," my father continued, raising his voice, "your memory fails you. I won that snuff box from you fairly, because your horse refused a water jump in Baltimore fifteen years ago."

Mr. Lawton made a grimace of impatience.

"Perhaps I can refresh your memory on a more immediate matter," he interjected harshly, "a matter rather more in keeping with your character. Don't, don't move, I beg of you! At a certain chateau in the Loire Valley, as recently as two months ago, you had an unfortunate escapade with French government agents."

"Let us err on the side of accuracy," said my father in gracious assent, "and add that the affair was rather more unfortunate for the agents than for myself."

"Meaning it was fortunate you ran away, I suppose," suggested Mr. Lawton, "fortunate, but natural. You escaped, Shelton, in the company of a certain young lady they were seeking to apprehend. You retained in your possession a list of names of political importance. It is a part of your damned blackmail, I suppose. I say you stole that paper!"

"Indeed?" said my father. "In that case, permit me! The snuff is excellent, Lawton, although the box is commonplace."

"By God!" shouted Mr. Lawton, "I've had enough of your damned simpering airs? You're a coward, Shelton. Why conceal it from me? A coward, afraid to demand satisfaction after a public insult—a thief with your theft still about you. I've come to get that list, to return it to its rightful owners. Try your drunkard's bragging on stupefied boys, but not on me! For the last time—will you give that letter up?"

My father's hand that held the snuff box trembled. His glance was almost furtive as he looked from Mr. Sims back to Mr. Lawton. For a moment he stared half-puzzled at Mr. Lawton's pistol. Then he moistened his lips.

"Suppose I should refuse?" he asked.

With a wan smile, Mr. Lawton rubbed his left hand over his long chin.

"In that case," he said, "I shall summon five men whom I hold outside. They will search the house, having searched you first. If they do not find the letter, I shall give you one more chance to produce it."

"Of course you realize your action is illegal?" my father interrupted.

Mr. Lawton laughed.

"We've beaten about the bush long enough," he said. "Will I have to remind you again that I didn't come to hear you talk? Come to the point. Will you give up that paper?"

With a sigh of resignation, my father fumbled in his breast pocket. When he spoke, it seemed a weak appeal to justify his action.

"Under the circumstances, what else can I do?" he demanded, "though it seems hard when I had given my word not to part with it."

He produced a long, sealed document, which he handed across the table. Mr. Lawton's eyes glistened with anticipation as he took it. He held it over the table to scan the seal.

"Damn all your caution, Sims!" he exclaimed exultantly. "We've got it just as I said we would! Didn't I tell you—"

His voice choked. He burst into a violent fit of sneezing. My father had thrown the contents of his snuff box into Mr. Lawton's face.

If his chair had been of hot iron, he could not have moved more quickly. Almost the same moment, Mr. Lawton's pistol was in my father's hand, cocked and primed and pointed at Mr. Sims.

"Brutus," said my father, "unburden Mr. Sims of his weapons. Lawton, a breath of night air may relieve you. Let us go to the window and reflect on the slip that may occur between the container and the nose. My son, give Mr. Lawton your arm. Assist me to open the shutters. Now Mr. Lawton, call to your men. Tell them they may go. Louder, louder, Mr. Lawton. Surely your voice has more strength. My ears have been weary this long time with its clamor."

CHAPTER V

EVEN TODAY, AS I pen these lines, the picture comes back with the same intensity, but little mellowed or softened with the years. The gaunt old room that had entertained so many guests, emptied of its last one, with nothing but the faint chill that had come through the opened window to remind one of their presence—the fitful light of the two candles that had begun spluttering in the tall brass sticks—Brutus with quiet adroitness clearing away the bottles and the dishes—and a sudden burst of flame from the back log in the fireplace that made his shadow jump unevenly over the opposite wall—and my father resting languidly in his chair again, quite as though nothing had happened—I remember looking about me and almost doubting that anything out of the ordinary had passed in the last five minutes. I glanced narrowly at him, but there was nothing in his manner to betray that he had not been sitting there for the past hour in peaceful meditation. Was he thinking of the other nights when the room was bright with silver and candles?

"My son," he remarked presently, "I was saying to you before our callers interrupted that there are just two things I never do. Do you still care to know them? I think that one may be enough for tonight. It is that circumstances oblige me to keep my word."

"You do not care to tell me any more?" I asked him.

"Only that you had better stay, my son. If you do, I can guarantee you will see me at my worst, which is better, perhaps, than hearing of me second hand. And possibly it may even be interesting, the little drama which is starting."

Thoughtfully he balanced the pistol he was still holding on the palm of his hand, and half unconsciously examined the priming, while I watched him, half with misgiving, half with a reluctant sort of admiration. When he turned towards me again, his eyes had brightened as though he were dwelling on a pleasing reminiscence.

"Indeed," he mused, "it might be more than interesting, hilarious, in fact, if it were not for the lady in the case."

"The lady!" I echoed involuntarily.

"And why not indeed?" he said with a shrug. "Let us do our best to be consistent. What drama is complete without a lady in it? It would have been simpler, I admit, if I had stolen the paper, per se, and not the lady with it. The lady, I fear, is becoming an encumbrance."

"Am I to understand you brought a woman with you across the ocean?"

He placed the pistol on the table before him, looked at it critically, and changed its position.

"A lady, my son, not a woman. You will find that the two are quite different species. I fear she had but little choice. That is a pretty lock on Mr. Lawton's weapon."

"You mean she is here now?" I persisted. He must surely have been in jest.

"To be sure!" he acquiesced. "She is, I trust, asleep in the east guest room, and heaven help you if you wake her. But why do you start, my son, does it seem odd to you that I should act as squire?"

"Not in the least," I assured him. "I am only astonished that she should consent to accompany you. You say, sir, that she is a lady?"

"At least," he replied, "I am broadening your education. That in itself, Henry, quite repays me for any trouble I may have taken—but I fear you are putting a bad construction on it. I beg of you, do not judge me so harshly. Launcelot himself—what am I saying?—Bayard himself, up to the present moment, could only commend my every action."

"Even to bringing her to this house," I suggested coldly.

"Precisely," he replied. "That in itself was actuated by the highest piece of altruism heaven has vouchsafed humanity—the regard a father has for his son."

"Do you mean to think," I demanded angrily, "that you can bring me into this business?"

I was still on my feet, and took a quick step toward him.

"Is it not enough to find you what you are? You've done enough to me tonight, sir, without adding an insult."

My father nodded, quite as though he were receiving a compliment. Seemingly still well pleased, he helped himself again to his snuff, and dusted his fingers carefully with his lace handkerchief.

"You misunderstand me," he said gently. "My present occupation requires a shrewder head and a steadier hand than yours."

"And a different code of morals," I added, bowing.

"Positively, my son, you are turning Puritan," he remarked. "A most refreshing change for the family."

I had an angry retort at the tip of my tongue, but it remained unspoken. For the second time that evening, the dining room door opened. I swung away from the table. My father leapt to his feet, bland and obsequious. A girl with dark hair and eyes was standing on the threshold, staring at us curiously, holding a candle that softened the austerity of her plain black dress. There in the half light there was a slender grace about her that made her seem vaguely unreal. In that disordered room she seemed as incongruous as some portrait from a house across the water, as coldly unresponsive to her surroundings. I imagined her on the last canvas of the gallery, bearing all the traits of the family line—the same quiet assurance, the same confident tilt of the head, the same high forehead and clear cut features.

Evidently a similar thought was running through my father's mind.

"Ah, Mademoiselle," he said swiftly in the French tongue, "stay where you are! Stay but a moment! For as you stand there in the shadows, you epitomize the whole house of Blanzy, their grace, their pride, their beauty."

She tried to suppress a smile, but only half succeeded.

"I fear the Captain has been drinking again," she said quietly. "Not that I am sorry. The wine improves you, I think."

"Mademoiselle lures me to a drunkard's grave," exclaimed my father, bowing low, "but pray be seated. A chair for the lady, my son. Early this afternoon they told me not to expect you. I trust you have had everything possible done for your comfort?"

For a moment she favored me with an incurious glance.

"I was unable to see you on the ship, captain, and I wanted to have a word with you at the first opportunity. Otherwise I would not have favored you with a tableau of the house of Blanzy. I wanted to speak with you—alone."

She had declined the chair I offered her, and was standing facing him, her eyes almost on a level with his.

"This," said my father, bowing again, "is delightfully unexpected! But I forget myself. This is my son, Henry Shelton. May I present him to Mlle. de Blanzy?"

"I suppose you may as well," she replied, holding a hand toward me indifferently. "Let us trust he has your good qualities monsieur, and none of your bad ones. But I wanted to speak to you alone."

"My son is discretion itself," said my father, with another bow. "Pray let him stay. I feel sure our discussion will not only interest but instruct him."

Mademoiselle frowned and tapped an angry foot on the floor.

"You heard what I said, sir. Send him out," she demanded.

"Stay where you are, Henry," said my father gently. "Stay where you are," he repeated more loudly, as I started for the door. "I have something further to say to you before you leave this house."

"Your pardon," he explained, turning again to Mademoiselle, "but my son and I have had a slight falling out over a question of ethics which I think directly concerns the matter you wish to discuss. Pray forgive me, Mademoiselle, but I had much rather he remained."

Mademoiselle glanced at me again, this time with an appeal in her eyes which I read and understood. It seemed to me a trace more of color had mounted to her cheeks. She seemed about to speak but paused irresolutely.

I made a bow which I did my best to render the equal of my father's, and for the first time I was glad I had entered his house.

"Mademoiselle," I said, "it is a pleasure to render you even so small a service."

And I turned to my father, and met his glance squarely.

"I cannot see any profit to either of us for me to remain longer," I observed, "either here or in this house," and I turned to the door.

"Brutus!" called my father sharply. "Stand by the door. Now sir, if you leave this room before I am ready, my servant shall retain you by force. Mademoiselle will pardon this domestic scene," he added, "the boy has an uncertain temper."

I looked to see Brutus' great bulk grinning at me from the doorway. I saw my father half smiling, and fingering the lace at his throat. I saw Mademoiselle watching me, partly frightened, but partly curious, as though she had witnessed similar occurrences. Then my pent up anger got the better of me. Mr. Lawton's pistol still lay on the table. Before my father could divine my intention, I had seized it, and held it pointed at Brutus' head.

"Sir," I said, breathing a trifle faster than usual, "I am not used to being threatened by servants. Order him to one side!"

My father looked at me almost admiringly, and his hand, that had been fingering the lace, groped toward an empty bottle.

"Anything but a bottle, father," I said, watching him from the tail of my eye, "anything but a bottle. It smacks of such low associations."

"Your pardon, Henry," he said quickly, "the movement was purely unconscious. I had thought we were through with pistols for the evening, and Mademoiselle must be fatigued. So put down the pistol, Henry, and let us continue the interview."

"Certainly," I replied, "as soon as you have fulfilled your part of the contract. As soon as you call off your servant, I shall wish you a very good evening. Stand where you are, Brutus."

"Come, come," said my father patiently, "we have had enough of the grotesque this evening. It is growing late, my son. Put down the pistol."

"Brutus," I called, "if you move again, backwards or forwards, I'll fire," and I backed towards the wall.

"Good," said my father. "Henry, you have an amount of courage and fore-sight which I scarcely expected, even in a son of mine, yet not enough fore-sight to see that it is useless. Put down the pistol. Put it down before I take it from you!"

His hand had returned again to his torn lapel, and he was leaning slightly forward.

"One instant, father!" I said quickly. "If you come a step nearer, I shall fire on your servant. Pray believe I am serious, father."

"My son!" he cried in mock alarm. "You distress me! Never be serious. Life has too many disappointments for that. Have you not read Marcus Aurelius?"

"Have you reloaded your snuff box?" I asked him.

"Not that," he said, shaking his head, "but I know a hundred ways to disarm a man, otherwise I should not be here witnessing this original situation. My son, I could have killed you half a dozen times since you have been holding that weapon."

"Admitted," I answered, "but I hardly think you will go to such lengths. We all must pause somewhere, father."

"No," he agreed, "unfortunately I am of a mild disposition, and yet—" he made a sudden move toward me—"Do you realize your weapon is un-primed?"

"Shall I try it?" I asked.

"Excellent!" said my father. "You impress me. Yes, I have underrated your possibilities, Henry. However, the play is over—"

He leaned towards the table abruptly and extinguished both the candles. The glow of embers in the fireplace could not relieve the darkness of the shuttered room.

"Now," he continued, "Mademoiselle is standing beside me, and Brutus is between you and me and approaching you. I think it would be safer if you put the pistol down. One's aim is uncertain in the dark, and, after all, it is not Mademoiselle's quarrel. Tell him to put down the pistol, Mademoiselle."

Her voice answered from the darkness in front of me.

"On the contrary," she said lightly, "pray continue. I have not the heart to stop it—nor the courage to interfere in a family quarrel."

"Quite as one would expect from Mademoiselle," his voice replied, "but fortunately my son also has not forgotten his manners. Henry, have you set down the pistol?"

I tossed it on the floor.

"Unfortunately," I said, "I have no woman to hide behind."

I hoped the thrust went home, but my father's voice answered without a tremor.

"You are right, my son. A woman is often useful, though generally when you least expect it. The candles, Brutus."

CHAPTER VI

HE RUBBED HIS FINGERNAILS on his sleeve and glanced about him with a pleasure he seemed quite unable to conceal. Mademoiselle's cold stare seemed to react upon him like a smile of gratitude. The contempt on my face he seemed to read in terms of adulation.

"Brutus, pick up the pistol. My son, you are more amusing than I had hoped. Indeed, Mademoiselle, perhaps the old saying is right, that the best is in our door-yard. I have had, perhaps, an exceptional opportunity to see the world. I have spent a longer time than I like to think collecting material for enlivening reminiscence, but I cannot recall having been present before at a scene with so many elements of interest. You harbor no ill feelings, my son?"

"None that are new," I said. "Only my first impressions."

"And they are—?" He paused modestly. He might have been awaiting a tribute.

"Father!" I remonstrated. "There is a lady present!"

"You had almost made me forget," he sighed regretfully. "You wished to have a word with me, Mademoiselle? I am listening. No, no, my son! You will be interested, I am sure. The door, Brutus!"

But it was not Brutus who stopped me. Mademoiselle had laid a hand on my arm. As I looked down at her, the bitterness and chagrin I had felt began slowly to ebb away. Her eyes met mine for a moment in thoughtful appraisal.

"You have been kind," she said softly, "Kind, and you know you have no reason—."

She might have continued, but my father interrupted.

"No reason," he said, "No reason? It is only Mademoiselle's complete disregard of self that prevents her from seeing the reason. A reason," he added, bowing, "which seems to me as natural as it is obvious."

I turned toward him quickly. From the corner of my eye I could see Brutus move nearer, and then Mademoiselle stepped between us.

"We have had quite enough of this," said Mademoiselle, and she looked from one to the other of us with a condescension that was not wholly displeasing. Then, fixing her eyes on my father, she continued:

"Not that I am in the least afraid of you, Captain Shelton. We have had to employ too many men like you not to know your type. Your son, I think, must take after his mother. I fear he thinks I am a damsel in distress. I trust, captain, that you know better, though for the moment, you seem to have forgotten."

"Forgotten?" my father echoed, raising his eyebrows.

"Yes," she said, speaking more quickly, "forgotten that you are in the pay of my family. You had contracted to get certain papers from France, which were in danger of being seized by the authorities."

Seemingly undecided how to go on, she hesitated, glanced at me covertly, and then continued.

"I accompanied you because—"

"Because you did not care to share the fate reserved for the papers?" my father suggested politely.

For a moment she was silent, staring at my father almost incredulously, while he inclined his head solicitously, as though ready to obey her smallest wish. Again I started to turn away.

"The door, Brutus," said my father.

"I am beginning to see I made a mistake in not remaining," Mademoiselle said finally. "Yet you—"

"Contrived to rescue both the papers and Mademoiselle, if I remember rightly," said my father, bowing, "an interesting and original undertaking, but pray do not thank me."

"Be still!" she commanded sharply. "You were not paid to be impertinent, captain. I have only one more request to make of you before I leave this house tomorrow morning."

He shrugged his shoulders, and glanced at me, as though definitely to assure himself that I was listening.

"I do not think that Mademoiselle will leave the house at that date," he said, with a second bow.

"And what does the captain mean by that?" she asked quickly.

"Simply that the house is already watched," said my father, "watched, Mademoiselle, by persons in the pay of the French government. Do not start, Mademoiselle, they will not trouble us tonight, I think."

For the first time her surprising self-confidence left her. She turned pale, even to her red lips, stretched out a hand blindly, and grasped the table.

"And the paper?" she whispered. "You have destroyed it?"

My father shook his head.

"Then," gasped Mademoiselle, "give it to me now! At once, captain, if you please!"

"Mademoiselle no longer trusts me?" asked my father, in tones of pained surprise. "Surely not that!"

"Exactly that!" she flung back at him angrily.

He bowed smilingly in acknowledgment.

"And Mademoiselle is right," he agreed. "I have read the paper. I have been tempted."

"You rogue!" she cried. "You mean—"

"I mean," he interrupted calmly, "that I have been tempted and have fallen. The document I carry has too much value, Mademoiselle. The actual signatures of the gentlemen who had been so deluded as to believe they could restore a king to France! Figure for yourself, my lady, those names properly used are a veritable gold mine, more profitable than my Chinese trade can hope to be! Surely you realize that?"

"So you have turned from cards to diplomacy," I observed. "How versatile you grow, father!"

"They are much the same thing," my father said.

"And you mean," Mademoiselle cried, "you are dog enough to use those names? You mean you are going back on your word either to destroy that list or to place it in proper hands? You mean you are willing to see your friends go under the guillotine? Surely not, monsieur! Surely you are too brave a gentleman. Surely a man who has behaved as gallantly as you—No, captain, I cannot believe it!"

"Mademoiselle," he said blandly, "still has much to learn of the world. Take myself, for instance. I am a gentleman only by birth and breeding. Otherwise, pray believe I am quite unspeakable, quite. Do you not see that even my son finds me so?"

He nodded towards me in graceful courtesy.

"For me," he continued smoothly, "only one thing has ever remained evident, and well-defined for long, and that, my lady, is money. Nearly everything else seems to tarnish, but still money keeps its lustre. Ah! Now we begin to understand each other. Strange you should not realize it sooner. I cannot understand what actuated so many persons, supposedly rational, to sign such a ridiculous document. That they have done so is their fault, not mine. I believe, Mademoiselle, in profiting by the mistakes of others. I believe in profiting by this one. Someone should be glad to pay a pretty price for it."

He stopped and shrugged his shoulders, and she stood before him helpless, her hand raised toward him in entreaty. For a moment my father glanced away.

"You couldn't! Oh, you couldn't!" she began. "For God's sake, Monsieur, think what you are doing. I—we all trusted you, depended on your help. We thought you were with us. We—-"

Her voice choked in a sob, and she sank into a chair, her face buried in her hands. My father looked at her, and took a pinch of snuff.

"Indeed," he said, "I am almost sorry, but it is the game, Mademoiselle. We each have our little square on the chess board. I regret that mine is a black one. A while ago I was a pawn, paid by your family. Then it seemed to me expedient to do as you dictated—to take you out of France to safety, to deliver both you and a certain paper to your brother's care. But that was a while ago. I am approaching the king row now. Forgive me, if things seem different—and rest assured, Mademoiselle, that you, at least, are in safe hands as long as you obey my directions."

He made this last statement with a benign complacency, and once more busied himself with his nails. I took a step toward him, and he looked up, as though to receive my congratulations.

"So you leave us, my son," he said briskly. "I fear you will meet with trouble before you pass the lane. But you seem surprisingly able to look out for yourself. Brutus will help you to saddle."

"You are mistaken," I said. "I am not leaving."

And I bowed to Mademoiselle, who had started at the sound of my voice, and was staring at me with a tear-stained face.

"I have decided to stay," I cried, "If Mademoiselle will permit me."

But she did not answer, and my father regarded us carefully, as though balancing possibilities.

"Not leaving!" Whether my statement was surprising or otherwise was impossible to discern. He raised his eyebrows in interrogation, and I smiled at him in a manner I hoped resembled his.

"I fear you may tire of my company," I went on, "because I am going to stay until you have disposed of this paper as Mademoiselle desires. Or if you are unwilling to do so, I shall take pleasure in doing it myself."

My father rubbed his hands, and then tapped me playfully on the shoulder.

"Somehow I thought this little scene would fetch you," he cried. "Excellent, my son! I hoped you might stay on."

"And now, sir," I said, "the paper, if you please."

"What!" exclaimed my father, with a gesture of astonishment. "You too want the paper! How popular it is becoming, to be sure!"

"At least I am going to try to get it," I began gravely, when a sudden change in his expression stopped me.

"Wait," he said coldly. "Look before you leap, my son. Allow me to make the situation perfectly clear before you attempt anything so foolish. In the first place, let us take myself. I am older than you, it is true, but years and excitement have not entirely weakened me. I have been present in many little unpleasantnesses. I have fought with Barbary pirates and Chinese junks, and with assorted Christians. The fact that I am here tonight proves I am usually successful. Even if I were alone, I doubt if you could take the paper from me. But you forget another matter—"

He turned and pointed to Brutus in the doorway. Brutus grinned back and nodded violently, his eyes rolling in pleased anticipation.

"Eight years ago," my father continued, "I saved Brutus from the gallows at Jamaica. He has a strangely persistent sense of gratitude. I have seen Brutus only last month kill three stronger men than you, my son. I fancy the document is safe in my pocket, quite safe."

He half smiled, and took another pinch of snuff.

"But let us indulge in the impossible," he continued. "Suppose you did get the paper. Let us examine the paper itself."

And slowly he drew it from his pocket, and flicked it flat in the candle light.

"Come, Henry, draw up a chair, and let us be sensible. Another bottle of Madeira, Brutus. And now, tell me, what do you know of French politics?"

"Sir," I objected, "it seems to me you are forgetting the point. What have politics to do with you and me?"

It seemed to me I saw another opportunity. With a sense of elation I did my best to conceal, I watched him quickly drain his glass, and I thought his eyes were brighter, and his gestures less careful and alert.

"Politics," he said, "and politics alone, Henry, are responsible for this evening's entertainment. Surely you have perceived that much. The glasses, Brutus, watch the glasses! These are parlous times, my son." He raised his glass again—

"Mademoiselle will tell you as much. We made an interesting journey through the provinces, did we not, my lady? It is a pity your father, the Marquis, could not have enjoyed it with us. He had a penchant for interesting situations, and in France today anything may happen. In a few scant months dukes have turned into pastry cooks, and barbers' boys into generals. Tomorrow it may be a republic, or a monarchy that governs, or some bizarre contrivance that is neither one nor the other. Just now it is Napoleon Bonaparte, a very determined little man. Ah, you have heard of him, my son? I sometimes wonder if he will not go further than many of us think."

Yes, we had already begun to hear his name in America. We had already begun to wonder how soon his influence would be overthrown, for it was in the days before he had consolidated his power. He was still existing in a maze of plots, still facing royalists and revolutionists, all conspiring to seize the reins.

"I sometimes wonder, Mademoiselle," he continued thoughtfully, "if your friends realized the task before them when they attempted to kill Napoleon. Ah, now you grow interested, my son? Yes, that is what this paper signifies. Written on this paper are the signatures of fifty men—signatures to an oath to kill Napoleon Bonaparte and to restore a king to France. You will agree with me it is a most original and intriguing document."

"So they didn't kill him," I said.

"Indeed not," he replied; "quite the contrary. They gave him a new lease of life."

"Then why," I demanded, "didn't they burn the paper. Why—"

"Ah!" said my father, with an indulgent smile. "There you have it, to be sure. You have hit the root of the whole matter."

"It was the old Marquis's idea. He told me of it at the time. If everyone in the plot signed the oath, it would be a dangerous thing indeed for anyone to inform on the rest, because they would immediately produce the paper which showed him as guilty as they. There are commendable points in the Marquis's idea, my son. Now that the plot has failed, the existence of this paper is all that keeps many a man from telling a valuable and dangerous little story. In these signatures I read names of men above suspicion, men high in the present government. Somehow Napoleon's police have learned of the existence of this paper. It has become almost vital for Napoleon to obtain it. He has tried to get it already. Since it reposed in the strong box at the Chateau of Blanzy, it has cost him five men. It has cost me new halliards and rigging for the Eclipse, and Brutus a disfigured countenance—not that I am complaining. Someone shall pay me for it. And the game is just beginning, my son. Mr. Lawton—have you wondered who he is? He is a very reckless man in the pay of France. He will get that paper if he can, if not by force, by money. Even now his men are watching the house. Suppose you held the paper in your hands, my son, you still have Mr. Lawton."

He folded the paper, and replaced it in his pocket.

"It is safer here at present," said my father. "There will be others who will want it presently, and then, perhaps, we will dispose of it."

"In other words, you intend to sell the people who entrusted you with the paper to the highest bidder?" I inquired.

He glanced towards Mademoiselle, and back to me again, and smiled brightly.

"That," he admitted pleasantly, "is one way of looking at it, though it might be viewed from more congenial angles."

I started to speak, but he raised his voice, and for the second time that evening became entirely serious.

"The paper," he said, "has nothing to do with your being in this house tonight. You are becoming more of a hindrance than I expected, but you are here, and here you will stay for another reason. I have heard much of the good examples parents set their children. For me to set one is a patent impossibility. I have never been a good example. But perhaps I can offer you something which is even better, and that, my son, is why I asked you to this house. Can you guess what it is?"

"There is no need to guess," I said, "you have been perfectly clear."

Gossip had it that my father always loved the theatre, though perhaps the Green Room better than the footlights. The marked passages in his library still attest his propensity. He now looked about him with a keen appreciation, as though my words were all that he required to round out his evening. Like a man whose work is finished, and who is pleasantly fatigued by his exertions, he leaned back in his chair.

"My son," he said, "you have a keenness of wit, and a certain decision, which I confess I overlooked in you at first—"

The moment must have pleased him, for he paused, as though on purpose to prolong it.

"You are right," he continued finally. "I am here to set you a bad example, Henry, and, believe me, it will be no fault of mine if it is not more effective than a good one. Listen, my son, and you too, Mademoiselle, I have been many things, tried many things in this life, most of them discreditable. I have wasted my days and my prospects in a thousand futilities. I have lost my friends. I have lost my position. Sneer at me, my son, laugh at me, curse me if you wish. I shall be the first to commend you for it. I am broad-minded enough to recognize your position.

"But above all things watch me. Watch me, and remember the things I do. Recall my ethics and my logic. They are to be your legacy, my son. What money I may leave you is doubtless tainted. But the things I do—of course you perceive their value?"

"Only in a negative sense," I replied pushing the bottle toward him.

"You are right again," he said, refilling his glass. "Their value, as you say, is purely negative. Yet, believe me, it does not impair them. You have only to place them before you and do exactly opposite. It is the best way I can think of for you to become a decent and self-respecting man. And now you have the only reason why I permit you in my society. The lesson has already started—an original lesson, is it not?"

As though to close the interview, he sprang up lightly, and bowed to Mademoiselle. It seemed to me he was combating a slight embarrassment, for he paused, seemingly uncertain how to begin, but only for a moment. Mademoiselle had regained her self-possession, and was regarding him with attention, and a little of the contempt which became her so well.

"Mademoiselle," he said, "even the pain of distressing you is lessened by the unexpected pleasure of your company tonight. I hope you have found the hour not entirely unprofitable. It has sometimes seemed to me, my lady—pardon the rudeness of suggesting it—that you may have seen something romantic, something heroic in me from time to time. I trust you have been disillusioned tonight. The fight on the stairs, the open boat—you see them all as they should be, do you not, the necessary parts of a piece of villainy? Pray forget them—and good night, Mademoiselle."

Suddenly both he and I started, and involuntarily his hand went up to cover his torn lapel. Mademoiselle was laughing.

"Captain," she cried, "you are absurd!"

"Absurd!" exclaimed my father uncertainly.

"You of all people! You cannot sell the paper!"

He sighed with apparent relief.

"And why not?" he asked.

"Because," said Mademoiselle, "you are one of those who signed it."

"Mademoiselle forgets," said my father, bowing, "that her name and mine were written at the bottom of the list. It is a precaution I always take with such little matters. The first thing I did, Mademoiselle, was to cut both off with my razor. Brutus, light the stairs for the lady."

Without another glance at either of us, she walked slowly away, her chin tilted, her slender fingers clenched. I knew that anger, fear, and disappointment were walking there beside her, and yet she left the room as proudly as she had entered it.

I stood listening to her step on the stairs.

"Ah," said my father, "there is a woman for you."

The last few minutes seemed to have wearied him, for he sank back heavily in his chair. For a minute we were silent, and suddenly a speech of his ran through my memory.

"May I ask you a question?" I inquired.

"It is my regret if I have not been clear," he said.

"It is not that," I assured him, "but you have appeared to allow yourself a single virtue."

He raised his eyebrows.

"You have admitted," I persisted, "that circumstances force you to keep your word."

"That," my father said, "is merely a necessity—not a virtue."

"Possibly," I agreed. "Yet, in your conversation with Mr. Lawton you stated that you had given your word not to surrender this paper. My question is—how can you reconcile this with your present intentions?"

For almost the only time I can remember, my father seemed puzzled for an answer. He started to speak, and shook his head—drew out his handkerchief and passed it over his lips.

"Circumstances alter even principles," he answered finally, "and this, my son, is one of the circumstances. Brutus, the boy has been trying to get me drunk long enough. Show him to his bedroom, and bring me my cloak and pistols."

Brutus lifted one of the candlesticks, grinned at me, and nodded.

"A very good night to you, Henry," said my father tranquilly.

I bowed to him with courtesy which perhaps was intuitive.

"Be sure," I told him, "to keep your door locked, father."

"Pray do not worry," he replied. "I have thought out each phase of my visit here too long for anything untoward to happen. Until morning, Henry."

"I am not worrying," I rejoined. "Merely warning you—pardon my incivility, father—but I might grow tired watching you be a bad example. Did you consider that in your plans?"

My father yawned, and placed his feet nearer the coals.

"That is better," he said, "much better, my son. Now you are speaking like a gentleman. I had begun to fear for you. It has seemed to me you were almost narrow-minded. Never be that. Nothing is more annoying."

I drew myself up to my full height.

"Sir—" I began.

He slapped his hand on the table with an exclamation of disgust.

"And now you spoil it! Now you begin to rant and become heroic. I know what you're going to say. You cannot see a woman bullied—what? Well, by heaven, you can, and you will see it. You cannot stand an act of treachery? Come, come, my son, you have better blood in you than to pose as a low actor. All around us, every day, these things are happening. Meet them like a man, and do not tell me what is obvious."

I felt my nails bite into my palms.

"Your pardon, father," I said. "I shall behave better in the future."

He glanced at me narrowly for a moment.

"I believe," he said, "we begin to understand. A very good night to you, Henry. And Henry—"

A change in his tone made me spin about on my heel.

"I am going to pay you a compliment. Pray do not be overcome. I have decided to consider you in my plans, my son, as a possible disturbing factor. Brutus, you will take his pistols from his saddle bags."

In silence Brutus conducted me into the cold hall and up the winding staircase, where his candle made the shadows of the newel posts dance against the wainscot. I paused a moment at the landing to look back, but I could see nothing in the dark pit of the hall below us. Was it possible I could remember it alight with candles, whose flames made soft halos on the polished floor? Brutus touched my shoulder, and the brusque grasp of his hand turned me a trifle cold.

"Move on," I ordered sharply, "and light me to my room."

My speech appeared to amuse him.

"No, no—you first," said Brutus. "I go—perhaps you be angry. See?"

And he became so involved in throes of merriment that I hoped he might extinguish the candle.

I thought better of an angry command, which I knew he would not obey, and turned through the arched moulding that marked the entrance to the upper hall, and at his direction opened a door. As I paused involuntarily on the threshold, Brutus deftly slipped past, set the candle on a stand, and bent over my saddle bags. Still chuckling to himself, he dropped my pistols into his shirt bosom. Then his grin died away. His low forehead became creased and puckered. He shifted his weight from one foot to the other irresolutely, and drew a deep breath.

"Mister Henry—" he began.

"Well," I said.

"Something happen. Very bad here. You go home."

His sudden change of manner, and the shadowy, musty silence around me threatened to shake the coolness I had attempted to assume. Unconsciously my hand dropped to the hilt of my travelling sword. I looked across at him through the shadows.

"You go home," said Brutus.

"Something *will* happen, or something *has* happened?" I asked.

But Brutus only shook his head stupidly.

"Very bad. You go home," he persisted.

"You go to the devil," I said, "and leave that candle. I won't burn down the house."

He moved reluctantly towards the door.

"Monsieur very angry," said Brutus.

"Shut the door," I said, "the draft is blowing the candle."

He pulled it to without another word, and I could hear him fumbling with the lock.

For the last ten years I doubt if anything had been changed in that room, except for the addition of three blankets which Brutus had evidently laid some hours before on the mildewed mattress of the carved four post bed. My mother must have ordered up the curtains that hung over it in yellowed faded tatters. The charred wood of a fire that had been lighted when the room was new, still lay over the green clotted andirons. The dampness of a seaside town had cracked and warped the furniture, and had turned the mirrors into sad mockeries. The strange musty odor of unused houses hung heavy in the air.

I sat quiet for a while, on the edge of my bed, alert for some sound outside, but in the hall it was very still. Then my hand fell again on the hilt of my travelling sword. That my father had overlooked it increased the resentment I bore him.

Slowly I drew the blade and tested its perfect balance, and limbered my wrist in a few idle passes at the fringe of the bed curtain. Then I knotted it over my hand, tossed a blanket over me, and blew out the light. From where I lay I could see the running lights of the Shelton ships swaying in a freshening breeze, three together in port for the first time in ten years. The sky had become so overcast that every shape outside had merged into an inky monotone. I could hear the low murmur of the wind twisting through the branches of our elms, and the whistle of it as it passed our gables. Once below I heard my father's step, quick and decisive, his voice raised to give an order, and the closing of a door.

Gradually the thoughts which were racing through my mind, as thoughts sometimes do, when the candle is out, and the room you lie in grows intangible and vast, assumed a well-balanced relativity. I smiled to myself in the darkness. There was one thing that evening which my father had overlooked. We both were proud.

He still seemed to be near me, still seemed to be watching me with his cool half smile. If his voice, pleasant, level and passionless, had broken the silence about me, I should not have been surprised. Strange how little he had changed, and how much I had expected to see him altered. I could still remember the last time. The years between seemed only a little while. We had been very gay. The card tables had been out, and he had been playing, politely detached, seemingly half-absorbed in his own thoughts and yet alertly courteous. I could see him now, pushing a handful of gold towards his right hand neighbor, and the clink of the metal and its color seemed to please him, for he ran his fingers lightly through the coins. And then, yes, Brutus had lighted me to my room. Could it have been ten years ago?

As I lay staring at the blackness ahead of me, my thoughts returned to the room I had quitted. Had she been about to thank me? I heard his slow, cynical voice interrupting me, and felt her hand drop from my arm. Then, in a strange, even cadence a sentence of his began running through my memory.

"It might be interesting, hilarious, in fact, if it were not for the lady in the case...."

CHAPTER VII

SOMETHING WAS PRESSING ON my shoulder, thrusting me slowly into consciousness. Half awake, I wrenched myself free, snatching for my sword as I did so. It was a chill and cloudy morning, and Brutus was standing by my bed, holding a bowl of chocolate between a thumb and forefinger, that made the piece of china look as delicately fragile as a flower.

"Eleven o'clock," he said. "You sleep late."

I looked at him blankly, still trying to shake off the drowsiness that crowded upon me. It seemed only a few minutes back that he had lighted me to that room. He must have detected a shade of suspicion in the look I gave him.

"Too much wine," said Brutus quickly.

But when he spoke, I knew it was not wine that made me sleep the whole night through. He thrust the bowl he was holding nearer to me.

"And now you poison me," I remarked, but he shook his head in emphatic negation.

"Hah!" he grunted, and emitted a curious chuckle that caused me to give him my full attention.

"You find the morning amusing, Brutus?" I asked.

He gulped and nodded in assent.

"Last night you kill me. Now I give you chocolate. He! He!"

I glanced at him over the edge of the chocolate bowl. It was the first time I had heard anyone laugh at so truly a Christian doctrine.

"Monsieur sends compliments," he said.

"Brutus," came my father's voice across the hall, "tell him I will see him as soon as he has finished dressing."

He was sitting before his fire, wrapped in a dressing gown of Chinese silk, embroidered with flowers. By the tongs and shovel lay a pair of riding boots, still so wet and mud-spattered that he must have pulled them off within the hour. A decanter of rum was near him on a stand. On his knee was a volume of Rabelais, which was affording him decorous amusement.

Brutus was busy gathering up the gray satin small clothes of the previous day, which had been tossed in a careless heap on the floor, and I perceived that they also bore the marks of travel. Careful mentors, who had taken a lively pleasure in their teaching, had been at pains to tell me that he was a man of irregular habits. Yet with indulgent politeness he remained blandly reticent. For him the day seemed to have started afresh, independent and unrelated to other days. It had awakened in him a genial spirit, far brighter than the morning. He greeted me with a gay wave of the hand and a nod of invitation towards the rum. My refusal served only to increase his courteous good nature.

"A very good morning to you, my son," he said. "So you have slept. Gad, how I envy you! It is hard to be a man of affairs and still rest with any regularity."

He waved me to a chair in a slow, sweeping gesture, timed and directed so that it ended at the rum decanter.

"You will pardon my addressing you through Brutus," he continued confidentially, "but it is a habit of mine which I find it hard to break. I am eccentric, my son. I never speak to anyone of a morning till I have finished my cup of chocolate. I have seen too many quarrels flare up over an empty stomach."

He stretched a foot nearer the blaze, and smiled comfortably at the hissing back log.

"And it would be a pity to have a falling out on such a morning as this, a very great pity, to be sure."

The very thought of it seemed to give him pause for pleased, though thoughtful contemplation, for he sipped his rum in silence until the tumbler was half empty.

"Once in Bordeaux," he volunteered at last, "there was a man whom I fear I provoked quite needlessly—all because I was walking in the garden with a headache, and my chocolate was late—Lay out the other shirt, Brutus, I must be well dressed today. What was it I was saying?"

"That you were walking in the garden with a headache," I reminded him. "Surely you had something better to walk with near at hand?"

He shrugged his shoulders, drained his glass, and wiped his fingers carefully on a cambric handkerchief.

"Either that or my conscience," he replied, "and oddly enough, I preferred the headache. He might have been alive today if I had had my chocolate. Poor man!" he sighed.

"You wanted to see me?" I asked, "or simply to impress me?"

He raised a hand in shocked denial.

"Pray do not believe I am so vulgar," he replied. "Yes, I wished to see you, Henry, for two reasons. First, I was absentminded last evening. I find I do not know the name of the gentleman with whom you had the falling out. If you tell me—who knows—the world is small."

He waited expectantly, and I smiled at him. I had hoped he would ask me.

"You really care to know his name?"

"It might be useful," he confessed. "As I said—who knows? Perhaps we may have something in common—some little mutual interest."

"I am sure you have," I told him. "The man I fought with was Mr. Lawton—at my uncle's country house."

For a fraction of a second I thought he was astonished. I thought that the look he gave was almost one of respect, but it was hard to tell.

"And you wounded him?" he asked quickly.

"I hardly think Mr. Lawton expected it," I acknowledged.

"I fear," he mused, "that the years are telling on Mr. Lawton—and your Uncle Jason knew of this unpleasantness?"

"Not until afterwards."

"Of course he was shocked?"

I nodded. "You had another reason for seeing me?" I asked.

"Yes," he replied, "a simple one. I did not want you to go downstairs till I went with you. Another cup of chocolate, Brutus. This morning, my son, I am consuming two cups of chocolate instead of one."

"You expect to find me irritable?" I suggested.

He shook his head in smiling contradiction.

"It is because I have a surprise in store for you. Who do you think has come to see me?"

"I am utterly at a loss," I said, bowing, "unless it is the constable."

"On the contrary," he replied, "it is the man I hate more than anyone else in the world."

Only his words, however, hinted that the contingency was unpleasant. His tone was one of pleased anticipation. He hummed a little tune, as Brutus knelt before him to help him on with a new pair of top boots, spotless and shining.

A few minutes later he stood before his mirror critically examining a coat of blue broadcloth. It evidently satisfied him, for he smiled back indulgently at his image in the glass, and watched complacently while Brutus smoothed its folds.

"A gentleman should always have twenty coats," he remarked, turning toward me. "Personally, I never travel with less than twenty-five—a point in my favor, is it not, my son?"

"And when we remember the lady who accompanies the coats—" I bowed, and he turned slowly back to the mirror.

"Let us trust," he replied coldly, "you will not be obliged to remind yourself often that she is a lady, and that she shall be treated as one both by you and by me as long as she remains beneath this roof."

I felt a pleasing sense of triumph at the success of my remark, and abruptly determined to drive it home.

"Sir," I said, "You astound me."

"Astound you?" He left his neckcloth half undone, and stepped toward me, alertly courteous. "You mean you take exception to what I have just said?"

"Indeed not," I replied, with another bow. "I find you changed this morning—into a good example instead of a bad one."

And then before he could reply, I leaned over the chair he had quitted. Lying in the corner of the faded upholstery was an oval of gold. Before he perceived my intention, I had picked it up, and almost at the same moment his hand fell on my arm. I looked up quickly. His face was close to mine, closer than I had ever seen it, placid still, but somehow changed, somehow so subtly different that I wrenched myself free, and stepped a pace away. Brutus dropped the coat he was folding, and shuffled forward hastily.

"How careless of me to have left it there," said my father gently. "Hand me the locket, if you please, my son, and many thanks for picking it up."

The jewelled clasp was under my thumb I pressed it, and the gold locket I was holding flew open, but before I could look further, he had struck a sharp blow at my wrist, and the locket fell from my hand.

"Pick it up, Brutus," he said, his eyes never leaving mine, and we watched each other for a second in silence.

"Come," he said, "let us go down stairs. You may find it instructive to see how I treat my enemies."

"I am afraid," I said slowly, "that you will do better without me."

Slowly the thin line of his lips relaxed, and he raised his hands to adjust his neckcloth.

"Your episode with Mr. Lawton makes me quite sure of it," he answered, in a tone he might have used to an ambitious school boy. "But you forget. You are still pursuing part of your education. Never, never neglect an opportunity to learn, my son. Something tells me even now you will be repaid for your trouble. Come, we are late already."

So I followed him down the, creaking stairs to the morning room. I could not suppress a start as I passed over the threshold. In front of our heavy mahogany table, attentively examining some maps and charts that had been scattered there, was my Uncle Jason.

CHAPTER VIII

OF ALL THE PEOPLE I had expected to see that morning he was the last. Almost unconsciously I recalled the little kindnesses he had rendered me. Busy as he had been with commercial ventures, there was never a time when he had not stood ready with his help. And even my father's name—he had never recalled it, except with regretful affection in his sad little reminiscences of older, pleasanter days.

I thought I detected a trace of that affection, a trace of appeal, almost, in the look he gave us as we entered. They made a strange contrast, my uncle, and my father, in his gay coat and laces, his slender, upright figure, and his face, almost youthful beneath his powdered hair. For my uncle was an older man, and years and care had slightly bowed him. The wrinkles were deep about his mouth and eyes. His brown hair, simply dressed, was gray already at the temples. His plain black coat and knee breeches were wrinkled from travel. As he often put it, he had no time to care for clothes. Yet his cheeks glowed from quiet living, and there was a sly, good humored twinkle in his brown eyes which went well with his broad shoulders and his strongly knit body. His reputation for genial good nature was with him still.

He stretched forth a hand, but the moment was inopportune. My father had given his undivided attention to the shutters on the east windows. He walked swiftly over and drew them to, snapping a bolt to hold them in place. Then he turned and rubbed his hands together slowly, examining my uncle the while with a cool, judicial glance, and then he bowed.

"You are growing old, Jason," he said, by way of greeting.

"Ah, George," said my uncle, in his deep, pleasant voice. "It does me good to see the father and the son together."

My father joined the tips of his fingers and regarded him solemnly.

"Now heaven be praised for that!" he exclaimed with a jovial fervor, "though it is hard to believe, Jason, that anything could make you better than you are. It was kind of you not to keep my son and me apart."

My father came a pace nearer, his eyes never for a moment leaving the man opposite. His last words seemed to make a doubtful impression on my uncle. He looked quickly across at me, but what he saw must have relieved him.

"Ah, that wit!" he laughed. "It has been too long, George, too long since I have tasted of it. It quite reminds me of the old days, George—with the dances, and the races and the ladies. Ah, George, how they would smile on you—and even today, I'll warrant! Ah, if I only had the receipt that keeps you young."

"Indeed? You care to know it?" My father quite suddenly leaned forward and tapped him on the shoulder. As though the abruptness of the gesture startled him, my uncle drew hastily back. And still my father watched him. Between them was passing something which I did not understand. The silence in the room had become oppressive before my father spoke again.

"Lead a life of disrepute," he said gravely. "I cannot think of a better cosmetic."

"George!" cried my uncle in quick remonstrance. "Remember your son is with you?"

"And seems amply able to look out for himself—surprisingly able, Jason. Have you not found it so?"

"Thank heaven, yes!" he laughed, and glanced hastily at me again.

My father's coat lapel was bothering him. He straightened it thoughtfully, patted it gently into place, and then said:

"Surely, Jason, you did not come here to discuss the past."

"Perhaps not," Uncle Jason replied with another laugh, which seemed slightly out of tune in the silence that surrounded him, "but how can I not be reminded of it? This room and you—indeed Henry here is all that brings me back. He is like you, George, and yet—" he paused to favor me with another glance—"he has his mother's eyes."

My father flicked a speck of dust from his sleeve.

"Suppose," he suggested, "we leave your sister out of the discussion. Let us come down to practical matters and leave the dead alone."

It was the first time he had mentioned her. His voice was coldly aloof, but his hand began moving restlessly again over his coat in search of an imaginary wrinkle.

"You understand me?" he inquired gently after a second's pause. "Pray remember, Jason, I have only two cheeks, and I can recall no biblical law to follow if you should strike again."

"God bless me!" gasped my uncle in blank amazement. "I did not come here to quarrel. I came because you are in trouble. I came as soon as I had heard of it, because you need my help—because—" he had regained his cordial eloquence from the very cadence of his words. He paused, and I thought his eye moistened and his voice quavered, "because blood is thicker than water, George."

At the last words my father inclined his head gravely, and was momentarily silent, as though seeking an adequate reply.

"I thought you would come," he said slowly. "In fact, I depended upon it before I set sail from France. Ha! That relieves you, does it not, Jason?"

Yet for some reason the statement seemed to have an opposite effect. My uncle's heavy brows knitted together, and his mouth moved uneasily.

"See, my son, how the plot thickens," said my father, turning to me with a pleasant smile. "And all we needed was a hero. Who will it be. I wonder, you or your uncle?"

But my uncle did not laugh again. Instead, he squared his shoulders and his manner became serious.

"It is not a time to jest, George," he said ominously. "Don't you understand what you have done? But you cannot know, or else you would not be here. You cannot know that the house is watched!"

If he had expected to surprise my father, he must have felt a poignant disappointment; but perhaps he knew that surprise was a sentiment he seldom permitted.

"I know," replied my father, "that since my arrival here I have been the object of many flattering attentions. But why are you concerned, Jason? I have broken no law of the land. I have merely mixed myself up in French politics."

Uncle Jason made an impatient gesture.

"You have mixed yourself up in such an important affair, in such a ridiculous way, that every secret agent that France has in this country will be in this town in the next twelve hours. That's all you have done, George."

My father tapped his silver snuff box gently.

"I had hoped as much," he remarked blandly. "When one is the center of interest, it is always better to be the very center. You must learn to know me better, Jason, and then you will understand that I always seek two things. I always seek profit and pleasure. It seems as though I should find them both in such pleasant company."

Then, as if the matter were settled, he looked again at the shuttered window, and leaned down to place another log in the fire.

"Come, George," urged my uncle. "Let us be serious. Your nonchalance and irony have been growing with the years. Surely you recognize that you have reached the end of your rope. I tell you, George, these men will stop at nothing."

"Has it ever occurred to you," returned my father, "that I also, may stop at nothing?"

My uncle frowned, and then smiled bleakly.

"No, George," he said, in a voice that dropped almost to a whisper. "You are too fond of life for that. Suppose for a moment, just suppose, they had means of taking you back to France. Just suppose there was a boat in the harbor now, manned and victualled and waiting for the tide, with a cabin ready and irons. They would admire to see you back in Paris, George, for a day, or perhaps two days. I know, George. They have told me."

"Positively," said my father, stifling a yawn behind his hand, "positively you frighten me. It is an old sensation and tires me. Surely you can be more interesting."

Jason's face, red and good-natured always, became a trifle redder.

"We have beat about the bush long enough," he said, with an abrupt lack of suavity. "I tell you, once and for all, you are running against forces which are too strong for you—forces, as I have pointed out, that will do anything to gain possession of a certain paper. They know you have that paper, George."

My father shrugged his shoulders.

"Indeed?" he said. "I hardly admire their perspicacity."

"And they will prevent your disposing of it at any cost. I tell you, George, they will stop at nothing—" again his voice dropped to a confidential monotone—"and that is why I'm here, George," my uncle concluded.

My father raised his eyebrows.

"I fear my mind works slowly in the early morning. Pardon me, if I still must ask—Why are you here?"

Quite suddenly my uncle's patience gave way in a singular manner to exasperation, exposing a side to his character which I had not till then suspected.

"Because I can save your neck, that's why! Though, God knows, you don't seem to value it. I have interceded for you, George, I have come here to induce you to give up that paper peacefully and quietly, or else to take the consequences."

Evidently the force he gave his words contrived to drive them home, for my father nodded.

"You mean," he inquired, "that they propose to take me to France, and have me handed over to justice, a political prisoner?"

"It is what I meant, George, as a man in a plot to kill Napoleon—" then his former kindliness returned—"and we cannot let that happen, can we?"

"Not if we can prevent it," my father replied. "If the trouble is that I have the paper in my possession, I suppose I must let it go."

Uncle Jason smiled his benignest smile.

"I knew you would understand," he said, with something I took for a sigh of relief. "I told them you were too sensible a man, George, not to realize when a thing was useless."

My father drew the paper from his breast pocket, and looked at it thoughtfully.

"Yes," he said slowly. "I suppose I must let it go."

"Good God! What are you doing?" cried my uncle.

My father had turned to the fireplace, and was holding the paper over the blaze. But for some reason my uncle was not relieved. He made an ineffectual gesture. His face became a blotched red and white. His eyes grew round and staring, and his mouth fell helplessly open.

"Stop!" he gasped. "For God's sake, George—"

"Stay where you are, Jason," said my father. "I can manage alone, I think. I suppose I should have burned it long ago."

He withdrew the paper slightly, as if to prolong the scene before him. If my uncle had been on the verge of ruin, he could not have looked more depressed.

"Don't!" he cried. "Will you listen, George? I'll be glad to pay you for it."

My father slowly straightened, placed the paper in his pocket, and bowed.

"Now," he said pleasantly, "we are talking a language I understand. Believe me, Jason, one of my chief motives in keeping this document was the hope that you might realize its intrinsic qualities."

Uncle Jason moistened his lips. His call was evidently proving upsetting.

"How much do you want for it?" he asked, with a slight tremor in his voice.

"Twenty-five thousand dollars seems a fair demand," said my father, "in notes, if you please."

"What!" my uncle shouted.

My father seated himself on the edge of the table, and surveyed his visitor intently.

"Be silent," he said. "Silent and very careful, Jason. You seem to forget that I am a dangerous man." And he flicked an imaginary bit of dust from his cuff. My uncle gave a hasty glance at the half opened door.

"And now listen to me," my father continued, his voice still gently conversational. "You have tried to frighten me, Jason. You should have known better. Of all the people in the world I fear you least. You forget that I am growing old, and all my senses are becoming duller—fear along with the rest. You have tried to cheat me of the money I have demanded, and it has tried my patience. In fact, it has set my nerves quite on edge. Pray do not irritate me again. I know you must have that paper, and I know why. The price I offer is a moderate one compared with the unpleasantness that may occur to you if you do not get it. Never mind what occurrence. I know that you have come here prepared to pay that price. The morning is getting on. You have the money in your inside pocket. Bring it out and count it—twenty-five thousand dollars."

Hesitatingly my uncle produced a packet that crackled pleasantly.

"There! I said you had them," remarked my father serenely. "All perfectly negotiable I hope, Jason, in case you should change your mind."

I stood helplessly beside him, beset with a hundred useless impulses. Silently I watched Jason Hill hold out the notes.

"And now the paper," said my uncle.

My father, examining the packet with a minute care, waved his request aside.

"First you must let me see what you are giving me. I fear your hands are trembling too much, Jason, for you to do justice to it. Twenty-five thousand dollars! It seems to me I remember that a similar sum once passed between us. In which direction? seem to have forgotten—Yes, strangely enough they are quite correct. A modest little fortune, but still something to fall back on."

"And now the paper!" demanded my uncle.

"Ah, to be sure, the paper," said my father, and he swung from the table where he had been sitting, and smiled brightly.

"I have changed my mind about the paper, Jason, and business presses. I fear it is time to end our interview."

"You mean you dare—"

"To accept a sum from you in payment of damage you have done my character? I should not dare to refuse it. Or let us put it this way, Jason. The paper is merely drawing interest. Positively, I cannot afford to give it up."

The red had risen again to my uncle's face, giving his features the color of ugly magenta. For a moment I thought he was going to leap at the slighter man before him, but my father never moved a muscle, only stood attentively watching him, with his hand folded behind his back.

"Show him the door, Brutus," he said briskly, "and as you go, Jason, remember this. I know exactly what dangers I am running without your telling me. For that reason I have ordered my servant to keep a fire burning in every room I occupy in this house. I make a point of sitting near these fires. If you or any of your friends so much as raise a finger against me, the paper is burned. And as for you—"

With a quick, delicate motion, he raised a hand, and drew a finger lightly across his throat.

"And as for you, Jason, even the slightest suspicion that you, or your paid murderers, are interfering in any way with my affairs, will give me too much pleasure. I think you understand. Pray don't make me overcome with joy, Jason; and now I wish you a very good morning."

But Uncle Jason had recovered from the first cold shock of his surprise. He drew himself up to his full height. His jaw, heavy and cumbersome always, thrust itself forward, and I could see the veins swell dangerously into a tangled, clotted mass on his temples. His fingers worked convulsively, as though clawing at some unseen object close beside him, and then his breath whistled through his teeth.

"You fool," he shouted suddenly, his temper bursting the weakened barriers of control. "You damned, unregenerate fool!"

And then, for an instant, my father's icy placidity left him. His lips leapt back from his teeth. There was a hissing whir of steel. His small sword made an arc of light through the yard of space that parted them. His body lunged forward.

"So you will have it, will you?" His words seemed to choke him. "Take it, then," he roared, "take it to hell, where you belong."

It was, I say, the matter of an instant. In a leaden second he stood poised, his wrist drawn back, while the eyes of the other stared in horror at the long, thin blade. And then the welts of crimson that had mounted to his face, disfiguring it into a writhing fury, slowly effaced themselves. His lips once more assumed a thin, immobile line. Again his watchful indolence returned to him, and slowly, very slowly, he lowered the point to the floor's scarred surface. His voice returned to its pleasant modulation, and with his words returned his icy little smile.

"Your pardon, Jason," he said. "I fear I have been too much myself this morning. Thank your God, if you have one, that I was not entirely natural. Take him away, Brutus, he shall live a little longer."

But Brutus had no need to obey the order. My father stood, still smiling, watching the empty doorway. Then I realized that I was very cold and weak, and that my knees were sagging beneath me. I walked unsteadily to the table and leaned upon it heavily. Thoughtfully my father sheathed his small sword.

CHAPTER IX

"The morning begins auspiciously, does it not, my son?" he said. "And still the day is young. Indeed, it cannot be more than eleven of the clock. The rum decanter, Brutus."

The lines about his mouth softened as his gaze met mine, and his smile grew broader.

"I pride myself," he went on, "that my example is all I promised. I fear I shall fall down in only one respect. Perhaps you have observed it?"

"If I have," I answered, "I have forgotten."

"My table manners," he said. "I fear they are almost impeccable." And he walked over to the window, taking care, I noticed, not to stand in front of it.

"Sad, is it not, that I should fail in such a trivial matter? But it happened so long ago while I was courting your mother, to be exact. My father-in-law, rest his soul, was an atrocity at table. The viands, my son, scattered from his knife over the board, like chaff before the flail. Yet, will you believe it? Any time he chose to speak his mouth was always full. I watched him, watched him with wonder—or was it horror?—I cannot remember which. And I resolved to go, to go anywhere, but never to do likewise. The result today is perhaps unfortunate. Yet watch me, my son, even in that you see the practical value of a bad example."

"Yes," I said, "I am watching you."

He seemed about to turn from the window, and then something outside held his attention.

"Ha!" he said. "A sloop is coming in—a clumsy looking vessel. Whose is it, Henry?"

I walked to the window to get a better look, but he reached out and drew me near him.

"Let us be careful of the windows this morning. The light is bad, and we have very much the same figure. There. Now you can see it—out by the bar. It carries too much canvas forward and spills half the wind. Have you seen it before, Henry?"

The sun had been trying to break through the clouds, and a few rays had crept out, and glanced on the angry gray of the water, so that it shone here and there like scratches in dull lead. The three ships near our wharf were tossing fitfully, and on all three, the crews were busy with the rigging. Out further towards the broad curve of the horizon was the white smear of a sail, and as I looked, I could see the lines beneath the canvas. He was right. It was a sloop, running free with the tide pushing her on.

"Yes," I said, "I know the boat, though I do not see why she is putting in."

"Ah," said my father, "and do you not? And whose boat may she be, Henry?"

"Two days ago she sailed from Boston for France. She belongs to Jason Hill," I told him; and, a little puzzled, I looked again at the low dunes and the marshes by the harbor mouth.

"I think," my father murmured half to himself, "that perhaps after all I should have killed him. Brutus!"

Brutus, who had watched the scene with the same aloof politeness that he might have watched guests at the dinner table, moved quickly forward.

"Has no word come yet?"

Brutus grinned and shook his head.

"The devil," said my father. "Aiken was here last evening, and got the message I left him?"

Brutus nodded, and my father compressed his lips. Apparently deep in thought, he took a few unhurried steps across the room, and glanced about him critically.

"A busy day, my son," he said, "a very busy day, and a humorous one as well. They think they can get the paper. They think—but they are all mistaken."

"You are sure?" I inquired.

"Perfectly," said my father. "I shall dispose of it in my own way. I am merely waiting for the time."

"Huh!"

Brutus cupped his great hand behind his ear, and nodded violently. My father stepped toward the hallway, and listened. Above the hissing of the fire I heard a voice and footsteps. He straightened the lace about his wrists, and his features lost their strained attention. As he turned towards Brutus, he seemed younger and more alertly active than I had ever known him.

"Ah, what a day," he said, "what a day, to be sure. They are coming, Brutus. Gad, but the years have been long since I have waited for them! Place the glasses on the table, Brutus. We still must be hospitable."

The knocker on our front door sent a violent summons, but my father did not seem to hear it. With graceful deliberation he was filling six glasses from the decanter.

"Keep to the back of the room, my son," he said, "and listen. Who do you think is coming? But you never can guess. Our neighbors, my son, our neighbors. First your uncle, and then our neighbors. We are holding a distinguished salon, are we not?"

But before I could answer or even conjecture why he should receive such a visit, my father gave a low exclamation, partly of surprise, and partly of well concealed annoyance, and stepped forward, bowing low. Mademoiselle, bright-eyed, but very pale, had run into the morning room.

"The paper, captain," she cried, "are they coming for the paper? For, if they are, they shall not have it. You—"

My father looked at her sharply, almost suspiciously.

"How are you here?" he demanded quickly, "Did not Brutus lock your door?"

"The lock was very rusty," she answered.

"Indeed?" said my father, "And how long ago did you find it out?"

"Only a minute back," she said, and again he glanced at her narrowly, and finally shrugged his shoulders. As I look back on it, it was his first mistake.

"Then I fear you have not seen much of the house," he said suavely, but she disregarded his remark.

"Pray do not be alarmed, my lady," "At almost any time I am glad to see you, but just at present—" he raised his voice to drown the din of the knocker—"just at present your appearance, I fear, is a trifle indiscreet. It is not the paper they wish, Mademoiselle. It is merely myself, your humble servant, they require. But pray calm yourself and rest assured they shall get neither. Let in our callers, Brutus."

He took her hand and bowed over it very low, and looked for an instant into her eyes, with a faint hint of curiosity.

"And you?" she asked. "You have it still?"

"Temporarily, yes," he answered. "Show Mademoiselle a chair, my son, over there behind me, where you both can witness the little drama. Perhaps it is as well she came, after all."

Brutus had not forgotten his days as a house servant. Erect and uncompromising he entered the room, facing toward us by the door.

"Mr. Penfield!" he called. "Captain Tracy! Captain Brown! Major Proctor! Mr. Lane! Captain Dexter!"

"So," said Major Proctor, "you still have your damned party manners."

They had entered the room, and stood in a group before my father. Their faces were set grimly. Their manner was stern and uncompromising, as befitted men of unimpeachable position and integrity. As I watched them, I still was wondering at their errand. Why should they, of all people have paid this call? There was not one who did not own his ships and counting house, not one who was not a leading trader in our seaport. In all the years I had known them, not one had looked at me, or given me a civil word, and indeed, they had little reason to give one. And yet, here they were calling on my father.

It was an odd contradiction of the lesson books that of all the men in the room, he should appear the most prepossessing. Though many of them were younger, his clothes were more in fashion, and time had touched him with a lighter hand. If I had come on them all as strangers, I should have expected kindness and understanding from him first of any. His forehead was broader, and his glance was keener. Indeed, there was none who looked more the gentleman. There was no man who could have displayed more perfect courtesy in his gravely polite salute.

"This," said my father, smiling, "is indeed a pleasure. I had hoped for this honor, and yet the years have so often disappointed me that I had only hoped."

Captain Tracy, short and squat, his hands held out in the way old sailors have, as though ready instinctively to grasp some rope or bulwark, thrust a bull neck forward, and peered at my father with little, reddened eyes, opened in wide incredulity.

"You what?" he demanded hoarsely.

"I said, Captain Tracy, that I hoped,"—and my father helped himself to snuff—"Will you be seated, gentlemen?"

"No," said Major Proctor.

"I have always noted," my father remarked, "that standing is better for the figure. The climate, Major, has agreed with you."

Major Proctor launched on a savage rejoinder, but Mr. Penfield leaned towards him with a whispered admonition.

"I take it," he said to my father, "that you did not read our letter. You made a mistake, Mr. Shelton, a grave mistake, in not doing so."

"I am fond of reading," said my father, "and I found your letter—pardon my rudeness—but I must be frank—I found your letter most amusing."

Mr. Lane stretched a claw-like hand toward him.

"You always did laugh," he cried shrilly.

"Never now, Mr. Lane," replied my father. "Yet I must admit, if laughter were my habit—" he paused and surveyed Mr. Lane's pinched and bony figure.

"You found the letter amusing, eh?" snapped Captain Tracy. "You found it funny when we ordered you out of this town, did you? I suppose you thought we were joking, eh? Well, by Gad, we weren't, and that's what we've come to tell you. Heaven help us if we don't see you out on a rail, you damned—"

"Gently, gently," interjected Mr. Penfield, in a soothing tone. "Let us not use any harder words than necessary. Mr. Shelton will agree with us, I am sure. Mr. Shelton did not understand. Perhaps Mr. Shelton has forgotten."

"My memory," said my father, "still remains unimpaired. I recall the last time I saw you was some ten years ago in this very house. I recall at the time you warned me never to return here. In some ways, perhaps, you were right, and yet at present I find my residence here most expedient. Indeed, I find it quite impossible to leave. Frankly, gentlemen, the house is watched, and it is as much as my life is worth to stir outside the doors."

"Good God!" cried Mr. Lane, in the shrill voice that fitted him so well. "We might have known it!"

There was a momentary silence, and Major Proctor whispered in Mr. Penfield's ear.

"Captain Shelton," said Mr. Penfield, "I see your son and a woman are in the room. It might be better if you sent them away. Your son, I have heard, has learned to behave himself. There is no need for him to hear what we have to say to you."

There was a note of raillery in his voice that must have offended my father.

"Mr. Penfield is mistaken. I fear closed shutters make the room a trifle dark to see clearly. It is a lady, Mr. Penfield, who is with us."

Captain Tracy laughed. My father's hand dropped to his side. For a moment no one spoke. Captain Tracy moved his head half an inch further forward.

"Well?" he asked.

"Let us leave the matter for a moment," said my father. "It can wait. Pray continue, Mr. Penfield. My son will be glad to listen."

Mr. Penfield cleared his throat, and looked at the others uncertainly.

"Go on, Penfield," said the Major.

"Mr. Shelton," began Mr. Penfield stiffly, "ten years ago you were a gentleman."

"Could it have been possible?" said my father with a bow.

"Ten years ago you were a man that every one of us here trusted and respected, a friend of several. In the War of the Revolution you conducted yourself like a man of honor. You equipped your own brig with a letter of marque, and sailed it yourself off Jamaica. You fought in three engagements. You displayed a daring and bravery which we once admired."

"Could it have been possible?" my father bowed again. "I do recall I failed to stay at home," he added, bowing again to Mr. Penfield.

Mr. Penfield frowned, and continued a little more quickly:

"And when you did return, you engaged in the China trade. You were a successful man, Mr. Shelton. We looked upon you as one of the more brilliant younger men of our seaport. We trusted you, Captain Shelton."

"Could it have been possible!" exclaimed my father.

"Yes," said Mr. Penfield in a louder tone, "we trusted you. You have only to look at your books, if you have kept them, to remember that."

"My books," said my father, "still contrive to balance."

"In the year 1788," Mr. Penfield went on, "you remember that year, do you not? In that year the six of us here engaged in a venture. From the north we had carried here five hundred bales of fur, valued at fifty dollars to the bale. You contracted with us, Captain Shelton, to convey those bales to England. It would have been a nice piece of business, if your supercargo had not been an honest man. He knew you, Shelton, if we did not. He knew the game you had planned to play, and though he was your brother-in-law, he was man enough to stop it."

Mr. Penfield's voice had risen, so that it rang through the room, and his words followed each other in cold indictment. The others stood watching my father with strained attention.

"Indeed," he said.

"Yes," said Mr. Penfield, "as you so aptly put it—indeed. Your ship carrying that consignment, had Jason Hill as supercargo, and Ned Aiken, that damned parasite of yours, as master. A day out from this port, a plank sprung aft, which obliged him to put back to Boston for repairs. The cargo was trans-shipped. When it was aboard again, Jason Hill happened to examine that cargo. The furs had gone. In their place five hundred bales of chips had been loaded in the hold. He went to the master for an explanation. Mr. Aiken, who had been drinking heavily, was asleep in the cabin, and on the table beside him was a letter, Shelton. You remember that letter? It bore instructions from you to scuttle that ship ten miles out of Liverpool harbor."

"And," said my father, with another bow, "I was to collect the insurance. It was nicely planned."

"If you remember that, you recall what happened next. We called on you, Shelton, and accused you of what you had done. You neither confirmed nor denied it. We told you then to leave the town. We warned you never to return. We warned you that we were through with your trickery. We were through with your cheating and your thieving. We warned you, Shelton, and now you're back, back, by your own confession, on another rogue's errand."

"Not on another's," my father objected mildly. "One of my own, Mr. Penfield. The experience you have outlined so lucidly convinced me that it was better to stick closely to my own affairs."

"Mr. Shelton," Mr. Penfield went on, regardless of the interruption, "we warned you yesterday to leave the town before nightfall, and you have failed to take our advice."

"I see no reason why I should leave," replied my father easily. "I am comfortable here for the moment. I would not be outside. Even the arguments you have given are specious. You got your furs back, and if I recall, they proved to be so badly moth eaten that they were not fit for any trade."

"Even though you see no reason," said Major Proctor smoothly, "you are going to leave, Shelton. You are going to leave in one hour. If you delay a minute later, we will come with friends who will know how to handle you. We will come in an hour with a tar pot and a feather mattress."

"You are not only unwelcome to us on account of your past," said Mr. Penfield, "but more recent developments make it impossible, quite impossible for you to stay. We have heard your story already from Mr. Jason Hill. You are right that it is no concern of ours, except that we remember the good of this town. We have a business with France, and we cannot afford to lose it. Major Proctor was blunt just now, and yet he is right. Give us credit for warning you, at least. You will go, of course?"

My father smiled again, and smoothed the wrinkles of his coat. For some reason the scene seemed vastly pleasant. He shrugged his shoulders in a deprecatory gesture, walked over to the table, and lifted up a glass of ram.

"I remarked before that I was quite comfortable here," he replied after a moment's pause. "I may add that I am amused. Since I have returned to the ancestral roof, and looked again at the portraits of my family, I have had many callers to entertain me. Two have tried to rob me. One has threatened me with death. And now six come, and threaten me with tar and feathers. Positively, it is too diverting to leave. Pray don't interrupt me, Captain Tracy. In a moment you shall have the floor."

He took a sip from his rum glass, watching them over the brim. And then he continued, slowly and coldly, yet turning every period with a perfect courtesy:

"There is one thing, only one, that you and all my other callers appear to have overlooked. You fail for some reason to realize that I do things only of my own volition. It is eccentric, I know, but we all have our failings."

He paused to place his glass daintily on the table, and straightened the lace at his wrist with careful solicitude.

"Once before this morning I have stated that I am not particularly afraid of anything. Strange as it may seem, this statement still applies. Or put it this way,—I have grown blase. People have threatened me too often. No, gentlemen, you are going to lose your trading privileges, I think. And I am going to remain in my house quite as long as I choose."

"Which will be one hour," said Major Proctor.

"Be careful, Major," said my father. "You have grown too stout to risk your words. Do you care to know why I am going to remain?"

No one answered.

"Then I will tell you," he went on. "Three of my ships are in the harbor, and times are troublesome at sea. They are armed with heavy metal, and manned by quite as reckless and unpleasant a lot of men as I have ever beheld on a deck. Between them they have seventeen guns of varying calibre, and there is powder in their magazines. Do I need to go any further, or do we understand each other?"

"No," snapped Captain Tracy hoarsely. "I'm damned if we do."

"It sounds crude, as I say it," he continued apologetically, "and yet true, nevertheless. As soon as I see anyone of you, or any of my other neighbors enter my grounds again, I shall order my ships to tack down the river, and open fire on the town. They have sail ready now, gentlemen. My servant has gone already to carry them my order."

"And you'll hang for piracy tomorrow morning," laughed the Major harshly. "Shelton, you have grown mad."

"Exactly," said my father gently. "Mad, Major. Mad enough to put my threat into effect in five minutes, if you do not leave this house; mad enough to scuttle every ship in this harbor; mad enough to set your warehouses in flames; mad enough even to find the company of you and your friends most damnably dull and wearisome; mad enough to wonder why I ever suffered you to remain so long beneath my roof; mad enough to believe you a pack of curs and cowards, and mad enough to treat you as such. Keep off, Tracy, you bloated fool!"

"By God!" Captain Tracy shouted, "We'll burn this house over your head. In an hour we'll have you shot against the town hall."

"Perhaps," said my father, "and yet I doubt it. Pray remember that I keep my word. Your hats are in the hall, gentlemen. In three minutes now my ships weigh anchor. If you do not go, I cannot stop them."

Mr. Penfield had grown a trifle pale. "Captain Shelton," he demanded slowly, "are you entirely serious? I almost believe you are. Of course you understand the consequences?"

"Perfectly," said my father.

"Let us go, gentlemen," said Mr. Penfield. "You will hear from us later." And he turned quickly towards the hall.

As he did so, my father drew back his right arm, and drove his fist into Captain Tracy's upturned face. His blow was well directed, for the captain staggered and fell. In almost the same motion he wheeled on Major Proctor, who had started back, and was tugging at his sword.

"Later, perhaps, Major," he said, without even lifting his voice. "But today I am busy. Pray take him away. He was always indiscreet. And you," he added to Mr. Lane, "surely you know well enough not to try conclusions with me. Take him away. Your hats are in the hall. I shall show you the door myself. After you, gentlemen."

And he followed them, closing the door gently behind him.

CHAPTER X

THE NEXT-TABLE CHAPTER X

MADEMOISELLE, WHO HAD RISEN from her chair, where she had listened, only half understanding the conversation in a tongue foreign from hers, stared at the closed door, her lips parted, and her forehead wrinkled.

"What have they been saying?" she asked. "Why are they afraid? Is everyone afraid of this father of yours?"

And then, impulsively, she seized me by the arm.

"But it makes no difference. Come, it is our one chance; come quickly, Monsieur. I must speak to you, where he will not disturb us."

"But where?" I asked, still staring straight before me; and then I noticed a bolt on the morning room door. I sprang toward it and drew it hastily. "It will do no good to talk, Mademoiselle. If you had understood—" And as I spoke, the enormity of the thing loomed still larger before me.

"Mademoiselle, this morning he has robbed my uncle of a fortune, snatched it from him here in this very room, and now he has threatened to move his ships into midstream, and to open fire on the town! And Mademoiselle, he means to do it. I thought once—but he means to do it, Mademoiselle."

She pursed her lips, and looked at me from the corner of her eye.

"Pouf!" she said. "So you are growing frightened also. Yet I can understand. The Marquis always said that Captain Shelton could frighten the devil himself."

"Frightened!" I echoed, and the blood rushed into my cheeks.

"Mon Dieu! Perhaps you are not. Listen, Monsieur, I am not taunting you. I am not saying he will not. He is serious, Monsieur, and you must leave him alone, or perhaps I shall not get the paper after all, and remember, I must have it. My brother must have it, and he shall, only you must not disturb him. He may shoot at the town, if he cares to, or murder your uncle. He has often spoken of it at Blanzy, but the paper is another matter. You must leave it to me."

"To you!" I cried.

"Precisely," said Mademoiselle. "You—what can you do? You are young. You are inexperienced. Pardon me, but you would be quite ineffective."

My cheeks flamed again. Somehow no sarcasm of my father's had bitten as deep as those last words of hers. I do not know whether it was chagrin or anger that I felt at the bitter sense of my own futility. And she had seen it all. As coldly and as accurately as my father, she had watched me, and as coldly she had given her verdict. She was watching me now with a cool, confident smile that made me turn away.

"Ah," she said, "I have hurt you, and believe me, I did not mean to."

Something in the polite impersonality of her voice gave me a vague resentment. She had moved nearer, and yet I could not meet her glance.

"I am sorry" she said, and paused expectantly, but I could only stare at the floor in silence.

"Believe me, I am sorry."

It might have been different if I had detected the slightest contrition, but instead I seemed only to afford her mild amusement.

"There is no need to be sorry," I replied.

"Ah, but there is!" she said quickly, "Last night you were very kind. Last night you tried to help me."

I seemed to see her again, standing pale and troubled, while my father watched her, coldly appraising, and Brutus grinned at her across the room.

"Mademoiselle" I began, "Anything that I did last night—"

"Was quite unnecessary," she said, "And very foolish."

I drew a sharp breath. The bit of gallantry I had on my mind to speak seemed weak and useless now.

"Mademoiselle is mistaken" I lied smoothly, "Nothing that I did last night was on her account."

"Nothing!" she exclaimed sharply, "I do not understand."

"No, nothing," I said, "Pray believe me, anything I did, however foolish, was solely for myself. I have my own affair to settle with my father."

"Bah!" cried Mademoiselle, tapping her foot on the floor, and oddly enough my reply seemed to have made her angry, "So you are like all the rest of them, stupid, narrow, calculating!"

"If Mademoiselle will only listen," I began, strangely puzzled and singularly contrite.

"Listen to you!" she cried, "No, Monsieur, I have listened to you quite long enough to know your type. I see now you are quite what I thought you would be. I say you are entirely ineffective, and must leave your father alone. You do not understand him. You do not even know him. With me it is different. I have seen the world. He is temperamental, your father, a genius in his way, and a little mad, perhaps. Leave him to me, Monsieur, and it will be quite all right. Last night, it was so sudden, that I was frightened for a moment. I should have remembered he is erratic and apt to change his mind. I should have guessed why he changed it. It is you, Monsieur. You have had a bad effect upon him. You have made him turn suddenly grotesque. What did you do to him last evening?"

"Do to him?" I asked, stupidly enough. "Why, nothing. I listened to him, Mademoiselle, just as I have been listening to him all this morning."

"And yet," she said, "it is your fault. Usually he is most well behaved. He is moderate, Monsieur. At Blanzy a glass of wine at dinner was all he ever desired. For days at a time, I have hardly heard him say a word. The Marquis would call him the Sphinx, and what has he been doing here? Drinking bottle after bottle, talking steadily, acting outrageously. What is more, he has been doing so ever since he spoke of returning home. I tell you, Monsieur, you must keep away from him, or perhaps he will do with the paper exactly what he says. Pray do not scowl. Laugh, Monsieur, it is funny."

"Funny?" I exclaimed, as stupidly as before. Mademoiselle sighed.

"If the Marquis had only lived—how he would have laughed. It was odd, the sense of humor of the Marquis. Strange how much alike they were, the Marquis and your father."

"It is pleasant that Mademoiselle and I should have something in common," I said.

Her gaze grew very soft and far away.

"Not as much as they had. We never shall. I think it was because they both were embittered with life, both a trifle tired and cynical. My father thought there should be a king of France, and yet I think he knew there could not be one. Your father—it is another story."

"Quite," I agreed. "And yet Mademoiselle will pardon me—I fail to see what they had in common."

"You say that," said Mademoiselle, "because you do not know him as well as I do. Do you not see that he is a bitter, disappointed man? They were both disappointed."

I examined the bolt on the door, and found it firm, despite its age. I glanced over the long, low studded room, and moved a chair from the center to a place nearer the wall. Her glance followed me inquiringly, but I forestalled her question.

"Mademoiselle," I observed, "was pointing out that she found something droll in the situation."

"And is it not droll you should have changed him?" she inquired, and yet I thought she looked around uneasily. "You have, Monsieur. He was cautious before this. He foresaw everything. He was willing to risk nothing. He even warned the Marquis against attacking the coach."

I began to perceive why the Marquis honored my father with his friendship.

"Was attacking coaches a frequent habit of the Marquis?" I asked.

"Has he not told you?" she exclaimed, raising her eyebrows.

"One would hardly call our conversation confidential," I explained. "Is that what you find so droll?"

And indeed, she seemed in a rare good humor, and inexplicably gay. A curious Mona Lisa smile kept bending her lips and twinkling in her eyes. The lowering clouds outside, the creakings of the beams and rafters under the east wind, nor even the drab gloom of her surroundings seemed to dampen her sudden access of good nature. The events she had witnessed seemed also to please her. Was it spite that had made her smile when she watched my father and his visitors? Was it spite that made her smile now, as she gazed at the room's battered prosperity, and at my grandfather's portrait above the mantlepiece, in the unruffled dignity of its blackening oils?

"It was the coach," said Mademoiselle, "of Napoleon at Montmareuil. A dozen of them set upon the coach. The lead horses were killed, and in an instant they were at the doors. They flung them open, but he was not inside. Instead, the coach was filled with the consular police. The paper, the paper they had signed, was at Blanzy, and your father had agreed to rescue it in case of accident. He would not leave me, Monsieur, and he would not destroy the paper."

She paused, and regarded me with a frown that had more of curiosity in it than displeasure.

"It was all well enough," she added, "until he heard of you, until you and he had dinner. It is something you did, something you said, that has made it all different. I ask you—what have you done to him? He was our friend before he saw you. Or why would he have ridden through half of France with Napoleon's police a half a league behind him? Why did he risk everything to bring out the paper when he might have burned it? Why did he not sell it there? He might have done so half a dozen times. Why does he wait till now?

"Do you know what I would say if you were older and less transparent? Do you know?"

An imperious, ringing note had entered into her voice, which made me regard her with a sudden doubt. About her was the same charm and mystery that had held me silent and curious, the same unnatural assurance, and cold disregard of her surroundings; but her eyes had grown watchful and unfriendly.

"I would say that you had turned him against us, and if you had—"

"Mademoiselle is overwrought," I said.

She tapped her foot on the floor impatiently, and compressed her lips.

"I am never overwrought," said Mademoiselle. "It is a luxury my family has not been allowed for many years. I say your father was an honest man, as men go, and a brave one too, and that you have changed him, and I warn you to leave him alone in the future. You do not know him, or how to deal with him. I tell you his trifling about the paper is a passing phase, and that you must not disturb him. No, no, do not protest. I know well enough you are not to blame. You must leave him to me. That is all."

"It pains me not to do as Mademoiselle suggests," I said.

"You mean you will not?" she flashed back at me angrily.

"I mean I will not," I answered with sudden heat, "No," I added more harshly, as she attempted to interrupt, "Now you will listen to me. You say I am a fool. You say I can do nothing against him. Perhaps not, Mademoiselle, but what I see is this: I see you in a dangerous situation through no fault of your own, and whether you wish it or not, I am going to get you out of it. He has done enough, Mademoiselle, and this is going to be the end. By heaven, if he looks at you again—"

"But you said—" she interrupted.

I did not have the chance to continue, for a hand was trying the latch of the door, and then a sharp knock interrupted me. My father was standing on the threshold. With a smile and a nod to me, he entered, and proceeded to the center of the room, while I closed the door behind him, and bolted it again. If he noticed my action, he did not choose to comment. Instead, he continued towards the chair where Mademoiselle was seated.

"I had hoped that you might get along more pleasantly, you and my son," he observed. "Surely he has points in his favor—youth, candor, even a certain amount of breeding. You have been hard on him, Mademoiselle. Take my word for it—he is to blame for nothing."

"So you have been listening," she said.

"As doubtless Mademoiselle expected," said my father. "I had hoped—"

"And so had I," I said.

He turned and faced me.

"Hoped," I continued, raising my voice, "that you might enter here, and leave your servant somewhere else. I have wanted to have a quiet talk with you this morning."

If he noted anything unusual in my request, he did not show it, not so much as by a flicker of an eyelash.

"It has hardly been opportune for conversation," he admitted. "But now, as you say, Brutus is gone. He is out to receive a message I am expecting, which can hardly be delivered at the front door. You were saying—Doubtless Mademoiselle will pardon us—"

"Mademoiselle," I went on, "will even be interested. I have wanted to speak to you so that I might explain myself. Since I have been here I fear I have been impulsive. You must lay it to my youth, father."

He nodded a grave assent.

"You must not apologize. It has been quite refreshing."

"And yet I am not so young. I am twenty-three."

"Can it be possible?" exclaimed my father. "I had almost forgotten that I was so near the grave."

"I came to see you here," I continued, "because, as my uncle said, you are my father. I came here because—because I thought—" I paused and drew a deep breath, and my father smiled.

"Why I came is aside from the point, at any rate," I said.

"Indeed yes," agreed my father, "and have we not been over the matter before?"

"If you had accorded me one serious word, it might have been different," I continued; "but instead, sir, you have seen fit to jest. It is not what you have done this morning, sir, as much as your manner towards me, which makes me take this step. That you have brought a lady from France and robbed her, that you have robbed my uncle, and have threatened to fire on the town—somehow they seem no particular affair of mine except for this: You seem to think that I am incapable of doing anything to hinder you, and frankly, sir, this hurts my pride. You feel that I am going to sit by passively and watch you."

I came a step nearer, but he did not draw back. He only continued watching me with a patient intentness, which seemed gradually to merge into some more active interest. His interest deepened when I spoke again, but that was all.

"You feel I am going to be still, and do nothing, even after you drugged me last evening. Did you think I would not resent it? You are mistaken, father."

My father rubbed his chin thoughtfully.

"I had not thought of it exactly so," he said, "yet I had to keep you quiet."

"So, if the tables were turned, and I were you, and you were I, you would hardly let matters go on without joining in?"

"Hardly," he agreed. "You have thought the matter out very prettily, my son. It is an angle I seem to have neglected. It only remains to ask what you are going to do. Let us trust it will be nothing stupid."

"I am glad you understand," I said, "because now it will be perfectly clear why I am asking you for the paper, and you will appreciate any steps I may take to get it."

He cast a quick glance around the room, and seemed satisfied that we were quite alone.

"Do I understand," he inquired, "that you have asked me for the paper?"

I nodded, and his voice grew thoughtfully gentle.

"You interest me," he said. "I have a penchant for mysteries. May I ask why you believe I shall give it to you?"

"I shall try to show you," I said, and tossed aside my coat and drew my small sword.

He stood rigid and motionless, and his face became more set and expressionless than I had ever seen it; but before he could speak, Mademoiselle had sprung between us.

"You fool!" she cried. "Put up your sword. Will you not be quiet as I told you?"

"Be seated, Mademoiselle," said my father gently. "Where are your senses, Henry? Can you not manage without creating a scene? Put up your sword. I cannot draw against you."

Mademoiselle, paler than I had seen her before, sank back into her chair.

"I am sorry you find yourself unable," I said, "because I shall attack you in any event."

"What can you be thinking of?" my father remonstrated. "Engage me with a small sword? It is incredible."

"I have been waiting almost twelve hours for the opportunity," I replied. "Pray put yourself on guard, father."

His stony look of repression had left him. The lines about his mouth relaxed again. For a moment I thought the gaze he bent upon me was almost kindly. Then he sighed and shrugged his shoulders, and began slowly to unwind a handkerchief which he had tied about his right hand, disclosing several cuts on his knuckles.

"I forgot that Captain Tracy might have teeth," he said. "Positively, my son, you become disappointing. I had given you credit for more imagination, and instead you think you can match your sword against mine. Pray do not interrupt, Mademoiselle," he added, turning to her with a bow, "it will be quite nothing, and we have neither of us had much exercise."

He paused, and carefully divested himself of his coat, folding it neatly, and placing it on the table. When it was placed to advantage, he drew his sword, and tested its point on the floor.

"Who knows," he added, bending the blade, "perhaps we may have sport after all. Lawton was never bad with the foils."

We had only crossed swords long enough for me to feel the supple play of his wrist before I began to press him. I feinted, and disengaged, and a second later I had lunged over his guard, and had forced him to give back.

"Mon Dieu!" exclaimed my father gaily. "You surprise me. What! Again? Damn these chairs!"

A fire of exultation leapt through me. I grinned at my father over the crossed blades, for I could read something in his face that steadied my hand. My best attack might leave him unscathed, but I was doing more, much more, than he had expected. I lunged again, and again he stepped back, thrusting so quickly that I had barely time to recover.

"Excellent!" said my father. "You are quick, my son. You even have an eye."

"Mademoiselle!" I called sharply. "The paper! In the breast pocket of his coat. Take it out and burn it."

"Good God!" exclaimed my father.

"You see," I said, "I have my points."

"My son," he said, parrying the thrust with which I ended my last words, "pray accept my apologies, and my congratulations. You have a better mind and a better sword than I could reasonably have expected. Indeed, you quite make me extend myself. But you must learn to recover more quickly, Henry, much more quickly. I have seen too many good men go down for just that failing. It may be well enough against an ordinary swordsman, my son, or even a moderately good one, but as for me, I could run you through twice over. Indeed I would, if—"

"The paper, Mademoiselle," I called again. "Have you got it?"

"Exactly," said my father. "The paper. If the paper were in my pocket, you, my son, would now be in the surgeon's hands. The paper, however, is upstairs in my volume of Rabelais. And now—"

His wrist suddenly stiffened. He made a feint at my throat, and in the same motion lowered his guard. As I came on parade, my sword was wrenched from my grasp. At the same time I stepped past his point, and seized him around the waist.

"You heard, Mademoiselle," I cried. "The door!" and we fell together.

My father uttered something which seemed very near a curse, and clutched at my throat. I loosened my grasp to fend away his hand, and he broke away from my other arm, and sprang to his feet. Just as he did so there was a blow, a splintering of wood. The door was carried off its hinges, and Brutus leapt beside him. The floor had not been clean. My father brushed regretfully at the smudges on his cambric shirt.

"My coat, if you please, Mademoiselle," he said. "I see you have it in your hands. Gad, my son! It was a nearer thing than I expected. On my word, I did not know that Brutus was back."

"He is like you, captain," said Mademoiselle, handing the coat to him. "You are both stubborn."

For some reason I could not fathom, her good nature had returned. It was relief, perhaps, that made her smile at us.

"It is a family trait," returned my father.

As though kicking down the door had been a simple household duty, Brutus turned from it with quiet passivity, and adjusted the folds of the blue broadcloth with an equal thoroughness, while my father straightened the lace at his wrists.

"Huh," said Brutus suddenly. Then I noticed that his stockings were caked with river mud, and that he had evidently been running. My father, forgetful of his coat for the moment, whirled about and faced him.

"To think I had forgotten," he cried. "What news, you black rascal?"

"Huh," said Brutus again, and handed him a spotted slip of paper. My father's lips parted. He seized it with unusual alacrity, read it, and tossed it in the fire. Then he sighed, like a man from whose mind a heavy weight of care has been lifted. The tenseness seemed to leave his slim figure, and for an instant he looked as though the day had tired him, and as though another crisis were over.

"He's there?" he demanded sharply.

"Huh," said Brutus.

"Now heaven be praised for that," said my father, with something that was a close approach to fervor. "I was beginning to wonder if, perhaps, something had happened."

Mademoiselle looked up at him demurely.

"The captain has good news?" she asked.

He turned to her and smiled his blandest smile.

"Under the circumstances," he said, "the best I could expect."

Still smiling, he smoothed his coat and squared his shoulders.

"Our little melodrama, my lady, is drawing to its close."

CHAPTER XI

THE SUN HAD FINALLY broken through the clouds, and already its rays were slanting into the room, falling softly on the dusty furniture, and making the shadows of the vines outside dance fitfully on the wall by the fire; and the shadows of the elms were growing long and straight over the rain soaked leaves, and the rank, damp grass of our lawn. It was the dull, gentle sunshine of an autumn afternoon, soft and kindly, and yet a little bleak.

"Yes," said my father, "it is nearly over. It turns into a simple matter, after all. I wonder, Mademoiselle, will you be sorry? Will you ever recall our weeks on the high-road? I shall, I think. And the Inn in Britanny, with Brutus up the road, and Ned Aiken swearing at the post boys. At least we were living life. And the *Eclipse*—I told you they would never beat us on a windward tack. I told you, Mademoiselle, the majority of mankind were very simple people."

"And you still feel so?" she asked him.

"Now more than ever," said my father. "I had almost hoped there would be one sane man among the dozens outside, but they all have the brains of school boys. No wonder the world moves so slowly, and great men seem so great."

And he wound the handkerchief around his hand again.

"The captain has arranged to sell the paper?" asked Mademoiselle.

"Exactly," said my father. "The price has been fixed, and I shall deliver it myself as soon as the day grows a little darker. I am sorry, almost. It has not been uninteresting."

"No," said Mademoiselle, "it has not been uninteresting."

"You are pale, my son," said my father, turning to me. "I trust you are not hurt?"

I shook my head.

"It is only your pride? You will be better soon. Come, we have always been good losers. We have always known when the game was up. Let us see if we cannot end it gracefully, as gentlemen should. You cannot get the paper. Why not make the best of it? You have tried, and tried not unskilfully, but you see now that the right man cannot always win—a useful lesson, is it not? I do not ask you to like me for it. You have seen enough of me, I hope, to hate me. And yet—let us be philosophical. Be seated, my son. Brutus, it is three o'clock. Bring in the Madeira, and the noon meal."

I did not reply, and he stood for a moment watching me narrowly. Brutus threw another log on the fire, which gave off a brisk crackling from the bed of coals. He then stood waiting doubtfully, until my father nodded.

"Take the door out as you go," my father directed. "Mademoiselle, permit me."

He pointed out an armchair beside the fire. "And you, my son, opposite. So." From the side pocket of his coat he drew a silver mounted pistol, which he examined with studious attention.

"Come," he said, slipping it back, "let us be tranquil. Is there any reason to bear ill will simply because we each stand on an opposite side of a question of ethics? If you had only been to the wars, how differently you would see it. There hundreds of men stab each other with the best will in the world, none of the crudeness of personal animosity, only the best of good nature. In a little time now we shall part, never, if I can help it, to meet again. You have seen me as a dangerous, reckless man, without any principles worth mentioning. Indeed, I have so few that I shall have recourse to violence, my son, if you do not assume a more reposeful manner. The evening will be active enough to make any further excitement quite superfluous. Have patience. An hour or so means little to anyone so young."

There fell a silence while he stood immovably watching us. A gust of wind blew down the chimney, and scattered a cloud of dust over the hearth. The rafters creaked. Somewhere in the stillness a door slammed. The very lack of expression in his face was stamping it on my memory, and for the first time its phlegmatic calm aroused in me a new emotion. I had hated it and wondered at it before, and now in spite of myself it was giving me a twinge of pity. For nature had intended it to be an expressive face, sensitive and quick to mirror each perception and emotion. Was it pride that had turned it into a mask, and drawn a curtain before the light that burned within, or had the light burned out and left it merely cold and unresponsive?

"The captain is thinking?" said Mademoiselle.

He smiled, and fixed her with his level glance.

"Indeed yes," he answered briskly. "It is a rudeness for which I can only crave your pardon. Strange that I should have tasted your father's hospitality so often and should still be a taciturn host."

Mademoiselle bit her lip.

"There is only one thing stranger," she said coldly.

"And that is—?" said my father, bending toward her attentively.

"That you should betray the last request of the man who once sheltered you and trusted you, and showed you every kindness. Tell me, captain, is it another display of artistic temperament, or simply a lack of breeding?"

Her words seemed to fall lightly on my father. He took a pinch of snuff, and waved his hand in an airy gesture of denial.

"Bah," he said. "If the Marquis were alive, he would understand. He was always an opportunist, the Marquis. 'Drink your wine,' he would say, 'drink your wine and break your glass. We may not have heads to drink it with tomorrow.' I am merely drinking the wine, Mademoiselle. He would not blame me. Besides, the Marquis owes me nothing. If it were not for me, your brother would be drinking his wine in paradise, instead of cursing at the American climate. And you, Mademoiselle—would you have preferred to remain with the police?"

He looked thoughtfully into his snuff box.

"Dead men press no bills—surely you recall the Marquis said that also. No, Mademoiselle, we must be practical to live. The Marquis would understand. The Marquis was always practical."

She caught her breath sharply, but my father seemed not to have perceived the effect of his words.

"Ah," he said, "here is Brutus with the meal."

Brutus had carried in a small round table on which were arranged a loaf of bread and some salt meat.

"Mademoiselle will join me?" asked my father, rubbing his hands. I do not think he expected her reply any more than I did. Indeed, it seemed to give him a momentary uneasiness.

"One must eat," said Mademoiselle. "We will eat, captain, and then we will talk." I am sorry you have made it necessary, but of course you have expected it."

"Mademoiselle has been unnaturally subdued," he replied. "It is pleasant she is coming to herself again. And you, my son, you should be hungry."

"As Mademoiselle says, one must eat," I answered.

"Good," he said. "The food is poor, but you will find the wine excellent," and he filled the glasses. It was a strange meal.

"Now we shall talk," said Mademoiselle, when it was finished.

My father raised his wine glass to the light.

"It is always a pleasure to listen to Mademoiselle."

"I fear," replied Mademoiselle, "that this will be the exception."

"Impossible," said my father, sipping his wine.

"All this morning I have tried to have a word with you," said Mademoiselle, "but your time has been well taken up. I hoped to speak to you instead of your son, but he failed to take my advice and remain quiet. As I said before, you are both stubborn. Not that it has made much difference. You still have the paper."

She caused, and surveyed him calmly.

"Is it not painful to continue the discussion?" my father inquired. "I assure you I have not changed my mind since last evening, nor shall I change it. Must I repeat that the affair of the paper is finished?"

"We shall see," said Mademoiselle.

"As Mademoiselle wishes," said my father.

"It has been six years since I first saw you in Paris," said Mademoiselle. Her voice was softly musical, and somehow she was no longer cold and forbidding. My father placed his wine glass on the table, and seemingly a little disturbed, gave her his full attention.

"Six years," said Mademoiselle. "I have often thought of you since then."

"You have done me too much honor," said my father. "You always have, my lady."

She only smiled and shook her head.

"You are the sort of man whom women think about, and the sort whom women admire. Surely you know that without my telling you. A man with a past is always more pleasant than one with a future. Do you know what I thought when I saw you that evening? You remember, they were in the room, whispering as usual, plotting and planning, and you were to have a boat off the coast of Normandy. You and the Marquis had ridden from Bordeaux. I thought, Captain, that you were the sort of man who could succeed in anything you tried—yes, anything. Perhaps you know the Marquis thought so too, and even today I believe we were nearly right. We saw you in Brussels later, and in Holland, and then at Blanzy this year. I have known of a dozen commissions you have performed without a single blunder. Indeed, I know of only one thing in which you have definitely failed."

"Only one? Impossible," said my father.

"Yes, only one, and it seemed simple enough."

A touch of color had mounted to her cheeks, and she looked down at the bare table.

"You have done your best, done your best in a hundred little ways to make me hate you. You have studied the matter carefully, as you study everything. You have missed few opportunities. Even a minute ago, about the Marquis—and yet you have not succeeded."

My father raised his hand hastily to his coat lapel.

"Is there never a woman who will not reduce matters to personalities," he murmured. "I should have known better. I see it now. I should have made love to you."

Though her voice was grave, there was laughter in her eyes.

"I have often wondered why you did not. It was the only method you seem to have overlooked."

"There is one mistake a man always makes about women." He smiled and glanced at us both, and then back at his wine again. "He forgets they are all alike. Sooner or later he sees one that in some strange way seems different. I thought you were different, Mademoiselle. Heaven forgive me, I thought you even rational. Surely you have every reason to dislike me. Let us be serious, Mademoiselle. You do not hate me?"

"I am afraid," said Mademoiselle, "that you have had quite an opposite effect."

In spite of myself I started. Could it be that I was jealous? Her eyes were lowered to the arm of her chair, and she was intent on the delicate carving of the mahogany. It was true then. I might have suspected it before, but was it possible that I cared?

"Good God!" exclaimed my father, and pushed back his chair.

Mademoiselle rested her chin on the palm of her hand.

"I told you the interview would not be pleasant," she said. "But you are pessimistic, captain. I have not said I loved you. Do not be alarmed. I was going to say I pitied you. That was all."

"Mon Dieu," my father murmured. "It is worse." And yet I thought I detected a note of relief in his voice. "Surely I am not as old as that."

Mademoiselle, whose eyes had never left his face, smiled and shook her head.

"I know what you are thinking," she said. "No, no, captain. It is not the beginning of a melodramatic speech. I am not offering pity to the villain in the story. Even the first night I met you, I was sorry for you, captain. I was sorry as soon as I saw your eyes. I knew then that something had happened, and when I heard you speak, I told myself you were not to blame for it. I still believe you were not to blame. You see, I know your story now."

"Indeed?" said my father. "And you still are sorry. Mademoiselle, you disappoint me."

"Yes," said Mademoiselle, "I heard the story, and I believe she was to blame, not you. After all, she took you for better or worse."

And then a strange thing happened. In spite of himself he started. His race flushed, and his lips pressed tight together. It seemed almost as though a spasm of pain had seized him, which he could not conceal in spite of his best efforts. With an unconscious motion, he grasped his wine glass and the color ebbed from his cheeks.

"Mademoiselle is mistaken," said my father. "Another wine glass, Brutus." The stem of the one he was holding had snapped in his hand.

"Nonsense," said Mademoiselle shortly.

My father cleared his throat, and glanced restlessly away, his face still set and still lined with the trace of suffering.

"Mademoiselle," he said finally, "you deal with a subject which is still painful. Pray excuse me if I do not discuss it. Anything which you may have heard of my affairs is entirely a fault of mine. You understand?"

"Yes," said Mademoiselle, "I understand, and we shall continue to discuss it, no matter how painful it is to you. Who knows, captain; perhaps I can bring you to your senses, or are you going to continue to ruin your life on account of a woman?"

"Be silent, Mademoiselle," said my father sharply.

But she disregarded his interruption.

"So she believed that you had filled your ship with fifty bales of shavings. She believed it, and called you a thief. She believed you were as gauche as that. I can guess the rest of the story."

But my father had regained his equanimity.

"Five hundred bales of shavings," he corrected. "You are misinformed even about the merest details."

"And for fifteen years, you have been roving about the world, trying to convince her she was right. Ah, you are touched? I have guessed your secret. Can anything be more ridiculous!"

He half started from his chair, and again his face grew drawn and haggard.

"She *was* right," he said, a little hoarsely. "Believe me, she was always right, Mademoiselle."

"Nonsense," said Mademoiselle. "I do not believe it."

My father turned to me with a shrug of his shoulders.

"It is pleasant to remember, is it not, my son, that your mother had a keener discernment, and did not give way to the dictates of a romantic imagination?"

"Sir," I said, "there is only one reason why I ever came here, and that was because my mother requested it. She wanted you to know, sir, that she regretted what she said almost the moment you left the house. If you had ever written her, if you had ever sent a single word, you could have changed it all. In spite of all the evidence, she never came fully to believe it."

"Ah, but you believe it," said my father quickly.

I do not think he ever heard my answer. He had turned unsteadily in his chair, and was facing the dying embers of the fire, his left hand limp on the table before him. Again the spasm of pain crossed his face. Mademoiselle still watched him, but without a trace of triumph. Indeed, she seemed more kindly and more gentle than I had ever known her.

"Five hundred bales of shavings," she softly. "Ah, captain, there are not many men who would do it. Not any that I know, save you and the Marquis."

"Brutus," said my father, "a glass of rum."

With his eyes still on the fire, he drank the spirits, and sighed. "And now, Brutus," he continued, "my volume of Rabelais."

But when it was placed beside him, he left it unopened, and still continued to study the shifting scenes in the coals.

CHAPTER XII

WAS IT POSSIBLE THAT I cared? There she was leaning toward him, the flames from the fire dancing softly before her face, giving her dark hair a hundred new lights and shadows. Her lips were parted, and in her eyes was silent entreaty. I felt a sudden unaccountable impulse to snatch up the volume of Rabelais, to face my father again, weapon or no weapon, to show her—

"Come, captain," said Mademoiselle gently. "Must you continue this after it has turned into a farce? Must you continue acting from pique, when the thing has been over for more years than you care to remember? Must you keep on now because of a whim to make your life miserable and the lives of others? Will you threaten fifty men with death and ruin, because you once were called a thief? It is folly, sir, and you know it, utter useless folly! Pray do not stare at me. It was easy enough to piece your story together. I guessed it long ago. I have listened too often to you and the Marquis at wine. Come, captain, give me back the paper."

With his old half smile, my father turned to her and nodded in pleasant acknowledgment.

"Mademoiselle," he observed evenly, "I have gone further through the world than most men, though to less purpose, and I have met many people, but none of them with an intuition like yours."

He paused long enough to refill his glass.

"You are right, Mademoiselle. Indeed, it is quite wonderful to meet a woman of your discernment. Yes, you are right. My wife called me a rogue and a scoundrel—mind you, I am not saying she was mistaken—but my temper was hotter then than it is now. I have done my best to convince her she was not in error. And now, Mademoiselle, it has become as much of a habit with me as strong drink, a habit which even you cannot break. I have been a villain too long to leave off lightly. No, Mademoiselle, I have the paper, and I intend to dispose of it as I see fit. Your mother, my son, need have had no cause for regret. She was right in everything she said. Brutus, tell Mr. Aiken I am ready to see him."

He must have been in the hall outside, for he entered the morning room almost as soon as my father had spoken, dressed in his rusty black sea cloak. At the sight of Mademoiselle, he bowed ceremoniously, and blew loudly on his fingers.

"Wind's shifted southwest," he said. "But we're ready to put out."

"Sit down, Mr. Aiken," said my father. "My son, pour him a little refreshment."

"Ah," said Mr. Aiken, selecting a chair by the fire, "pour it out, my lad—fill her up. It's a short life and little joy, 'less we draw it from the bottle. And long life and much joy to you, sir, by the same token," he added, raising his glass and tossing the spirits adroitly down his throat. Then, with a comfortable sigh, he drew out his pipe and lighted it on an ember.

"Yes, she'll be blowing before morning."

"You don't mean," inquired my father, with a glance out of the window, "that I can't launch a small boat from the beach?"

"You could, captain, if you'd a mind to," said Ned Aiken, tamping down his tobacco, "but there's lots who couldn't."

"Then I shall," said my father languidly. "Brutus and I will board the *Sea Tern* at eight o'clock tonight. You will stand off outside and put on your running lights."

"Yes," said Mr. Aiken, "it's time we was going."

"You mean they are taking steps?"

"A frigate's due in at midnight," said Mr. Aiken, grinning.

"A frigate! Think of that!" said my father. "At last we seem to be making our mark on the world."

"We've never done the beat of this," said Mr. Aiken.

"And everything is quiet outside?"

"All right so far," said Mr. Aiken.

"How many men are watching the house?"

"There's four, sir," he answered.

"Ah," said my father, "and Mr. Lawton still stops at the tavern?"

"Hasn't showed his head all morning," answered Mr. Aiken.

"Ah," said my father, "perhaps he is right in concealing such a useless member." And he helped himself from the decanter, seemed to hesitate for a moment, and continued:

"And Mr. Jason Hill—he has been to call, Ned. Have you seen him since?"

"He's been walking out in the road, sir, all morning," replied Mr. Aiken. "And a schooner of his is anchored upstream. And if you'll pardon the liberty, I don't give that for Jason Hill," and he spat into the fire.

"It may please you to know," said my father, "that I quite agree with you. I am afraid," he went on, looking at the back of his hand, "that Jason does not take me seriously. I fear he will find he is wrong. Brutus!"

Brutus, apparently anticipating something pleasant, moved towards my father's chair.

"My pistols, Brutus. And it is growing dark. You had best draw the shutters and bring in the candles. We're sailing very close to the wind this evening. Listen to me carefully, Brutus. You will have the cutter by the bar at eight o'clock, and in five minutes you will bring out my horse."

"What's the horse for?" asked Mr. Aiken.

My father settled himself back more comfortably in his chair before he answered. A few drops of wine had spilled on the mahogany. He touched them, and held up his fingers and looked thoughtfully at the stain.

"Because I propose to ride through them," he said. "I propose showing our friends—how shall I put it so you'll understand?—that I don't care a damn for the whole pack."

"Gad!" murmured Mr. Aiken. "I might have known it. And here I was thinking you'd be quiet and sensible. Are you still going on with that damned paper?"

The red of the wine seemed to please my father. He dipped his fingers in it again and drew them slowly across the back of his left hand.

"Precisely," he said. "I propose to deliver it tonight before I sail. I leave it at Hixon's farm."

"He's dead," said Mr. Aiken.

"Exactly," said my father. "Only his shade will help me. Perhaps it will be enough—who knows?"

"There'll be half a dozen after you before you get through the gate," said Mr. Aiken dubiously. "You can lay to it Lawton will be there before you make a turn."

"That," said my father, "is why I say we're sailing very close to the wind."

"Good God, sir, burn it up," said Mr. Aiken plaintively. "What's it been doing but causing trouble ever since we've got it? Running gear carried away—man wounded from splinters. Hell to pay everywhere. Gad, sir, they're afraid to sleep tonight for fear you'll blow 'em out of bed. What's the use of it all? Damn it, that's what I say, what's the use? And now here you go, risking getting a piece of lead thrown in you, all because of a few names scrawled on a piece of paper. Here it's the first time you've been back. It's a hell of a home-coming—that's what I say. I told you you hadn't ought to have come. Now there's the fire. Why not forget it and burn it up, and then it's over just as neat as neat, and then we're aboard, and after the pearls again. Why, what must the boy be thinking of all this? He must be thinking he's got a hell-cat for a father. That's what he must be thinking."

"That will do," said my father coldly, and he rose slowly from his chair, and stood squarely in front of me.

"Tie that boy up, Brutus," he commanded. "It is a compliment, my son. My opinion of you is steadily rising. Tie him up, Brutus. You will find a rope on the chimney piece."

He stood close to me, evidently pleased at the convulsive anger which had gripped me. Brutus was still fumbling on the mantlepiece. Ned Aiken's pipe had dropped from his mouth. It was Mademoiselle who was the first to intervene.

"Are you out of your senses?" she demanded, seizing him by the arm. "It is too much, captain, I tell you it is too much. Think what you are doing, and send the black man off."

"I have been thinking the matter over for some time," replied my father tranquilly, "and I have determined to do the thing thoroughly. If he cannot like me, it is better for him to hate me, and may save trouble. Tie him up, Brutus."

"Bear away!" cried Mr. Aiken harshly. "Mind yourself, sir."

His warning, however, was late in coming. I had sprung at my father before the sentence was finished. It was almost the only time I knew him to miscalculate. He must have been taken unaware, for he stepped backward too quickly, and collided with the very chair he had quitted. It shook his balance for the moment, so that he thrust a hand behind him to recover himself, and in the same instant I had the volume of Rabelais. I leapt for the open doorway, but Ned Aiken was there to intercept me. Brutus was up behind me with his great hands clamping down on my shoulders. I turned and hurled the volume in the fireplace.

My father caught it out almost before it landed. With all the deliberation of a connoisseur examining an old and rare edition, he turned the pages with his slim fingers. There, as he had said, was the paper, with the same red seals that I had admired the previous evening. He placed it slowly in his inside pocket, and tossed the book on the floor.

"Now here's a pretty kettle of fish," said Mr. Aiken.

My father was watching me thoughtfully.

"Take your hands off him, Brutus," he said, "and bring out the horse."

For a second longer we stood motionless, each watching the other. Then my father crossed to the long table near which I was standing, picked up the pistols that Brutus had left there, and slipped them into his capacious side pockets.

"You disappoint me, Henry," he remarked. "You should have used those pistols."

"I had thought of them," I answered.

"I am glad of that," he said. "It is a relief to know you did not overlook them. You were right, Mademoiselle. I should have known better than to treat him so. We have ceased to play the game, my son. It only remains to take my leave. I shall not trouble you again."

He was standing close beside me. Was it possible his eyes were a little wistful, and his voice a trifle sad?

"I thought I should be glad to leave you," he said, "and somehow I am sorry. Odd that we can never properly gauge our emotions. I feel that you will be a very blithe and active gentleman in time, and there are not so many left in these drab days. Ah, well—"

His sword was lying on the table. He drew it, and tucked the naked blade under his arm. In spite of the two candles which Brutus had left, the shadows had closed about us, so that his figure alone remained distinct in the yellow light, slender and carelessly elegant. I think it pleased him to have us all three watching. Any gathering, however small, that he might dominate, appeared to give him enjoyment—his leave taking not less than the others.

"It is growing dark, Mr. Aiken," he observed, "and our position is not without its drawbacks. Call in the men from outside, and take them aboard and give them a measure of rum. No one will disturb me before I leave, I think. You had better weigh at once, and never mind your running lights till it is time for them."

"So you're going to do it," said Mr. Aiken. "I might have known you wouldn't listen to reason."

"You should have sailed with me long enough," said my father, "to know I never do."

"And you not even dressed for it," added Mr. Aiken. "You might be going to a party, so you might."

"I think," replied my father, "the evening will be more interesting than a purely social affair. Keep the *Sea Tern* well off, and we shall meet only too soon again.'

"Why don't I take the boy along," Mr. Aiken suggested, eyeing me a little furtively. "He'd be right useful where we're going, and the sea would do him good, so it would."

"I fancy you'll have enough bother without him," replied my father. "Personally I have found him quite distracting during my short visit."

"Hell," said Mr. Aiken, "he wouldn't be no trouble, but he looks fair ugly here, so he does, and he knows too much. No offense, sir, but he's too up and coming to be left alone with an ignorant negro."

My father shrugged.

"Brutus is fond of the boy. He will not hurt him."

"But the boy might hurt the negro," said Mr. Aiken.

My father nodded blandly toward the hall.

"And you might be seasick," he said.

"Har," roared Mr. Aiken, seemingly struck by the subtle humor of the remark. "Damned if you wouldn't joke if the deck was blowing off under you. Damned if I ever seen the likes of you now, captain."

Still under the spell of mirth he left us. The house door closed behind him, and Brutus glided into the room.

"Mademoiselle," said my father bowing, "I am sorry the cards have fallen so we must part. If you had as few pleasant things as I to remember, you also might understand how poignantly I regret it, even though I know it is for the best. It is time you were leaving such low company."

"I have found it pleasant sometimes," she replied a little wistfully. "It takes very little to please me, captain."

"Sometimes," he replied, smiling, "anything is pleasant, but only sometimes. Your brother has been notified, Mademoiselle. You should hear from him in a little while now, when this hurry and bustle is over, and when you see him, give him my regards and my regrets. And Mademoiselle" —he hesitated an instant—"would you think it insolent if I said I sometimes wished—Mon Dieu, Mademoiselle, do not take it so. It was entirely unpardonable of me."

Mademoiselle had hidden her face in her hands. My father, frowning slightly, rubbed his thumb along his sword blade.

"Forgive me, if you can," he said. "I have often feared my manners would fail me sometime."

She looked up at him then, and her eyes were very bright.

"Suppose," she said softly, "I told you there was nothing to forgive. Suppose I said—"

My father, bowing his lowest, politely and rather hastily interrupted.

"Mademoiselle would be too kind. She would have forgotten that it is quite impossible."

"No," said Mademoiselle, shaking her head slowly, "it is not impossible. You should have known better than to say that. Suppose—" her voice choked a little, as though the words hurt her—"suppose I bade you recall, captain, what you said on the stairs at Blanzy, when they were at the door and you were going to meet them. Do you remember?"

My father smiled, and made a polite little gesture of assumed despair. Then his voice, very slow and cool, broke in on her speech and stilled it.

"Good God, Mademoiselle, one cannot remember everything."

Playing with the hilt of his sword, he stepped nearer, still smiling, still watching her with a polished curiosity.

"I have said so many little things to women in my time, so many little nothings. It is hard to remember them all. They have become confused now, and blended into an interesting background, whose elements I can no longer separate. Your pardon, my lady, but I have forgotten, forgotten so completely that even the stairs seem merely a gentle blur."

And he pressed his hand over his brow and sighed, while he watched her face flush crimson.

"You lie!" she cried. "You have not forgotten!"

My father ceased to smile.

"And suppose I have not," he said. "What is it to Mademoiselle? What are the words of a ruined man, the idle speech of a fool who fancied he would sup that night in paradise, and what use is it to recall them now? Is it possible you believe I am touched by such trivial matters? Because everyone had done what you wish, do you think I shall also? Do you think you can make me give up the paper, as though I were a simpering, romantic fool in Paris? Do you think I have gone this far to turn back? Mademoiselle seems to forget that I have the game in my own hands. It would be a foolish thing to throw it all away, even—"

He paused, and bowed again.

"Even for you, Mademoiselle. I have arrived where I am today only for one reason. Can you not guess it? It was a pleasure to take you from Blanzy. It is business now, and they cannot be combined.

"Listen, Mademoiselle," he continued. "Not three miles off the harbor mouth is a French ship tacking back and forth, and not entirely for pleasure. Around this house at present are enough men to run your estates at Blanzy. A sloop has come into the harbor this morning, and has landed its crew for my especial benefit. A dozen of Napoleon's agents are waiting to spring at my throat. I have succeeded so that there is not a man in town who would not be glad to see me on a yard arm. And yet they are waiting, Mademoiselle. Is it not amusing? Can you guess why they are waiting?"

He took a pinch of snuff and dusted his fingers.

"Because they fear that I may burn the paper if they disturb me. They believe if they keep hidden, if I do not suspect, that I may venture forth. They hope to take me alive, or kill me, and still obtain the paper. Indeed, it is their one hope. It would be a pity to disappoint them."

His lips had parted, and his eyes were shining in the candle light.

"There are few things which move me now, my lady. All that I really enjoy is an amusing situation, and this one is very amusing. Do you think I have crossed the ocean to deliver this document, and then I shall stop? No, Mademoiselle, you are mistaken."

He bowed again, and stepped backwards towards the door.

"Pray do likewise, Mademoiselle, and forget," he said. "There is nothing in this little episode fit for you to remember. It is not you they are after, and you will be quite safe here. I have made sure of that. My son will remain until your brother arrives, and will dispense what hospitality you require.

"I trust," he added, turning to me, "you still remember why you have been here?"

"Indeed, yes," I answered.

"Then it is good-bye, Henry. I shall not bother to offer you my hand. Brutus, you will remain with my son until a quarter to seven."

Even now I cannot tell what made a mist come over my eyes and a lump in my throat any more than I can explain my subsequent actions on that evening. Was it possible I was sorry to see the last of him? Or was it simply self pity that shortened my breath and made my voice seem broken and discordant?

"And after that?" I asked.

He looked at me appraisingly, tapping his thin fingers on his sword hilt.

"After that—" He stared thoughtfully at the shadows of the darkened room. Was he thinking as I was, of the wasted years and what the end would be?

"After that," he repeated, half to himself, "come, I will make an appointment with you after that—on the other side of the Styx, my son. I shall be waiting there, I promise you, and we shall drink some corked ambrosia. Surely the gods must give a little to the shades, or at any rate, Brutus shall steal some. And then perhaps you shall tell me what happened after that. I shall look forward—I shall hope, even, that it may be pleasant. Good-bye, my son."

I think he had often planned that leave taking. Surely it must have satisfied him.

CHAPTER XIII

HE WAS GONE, LIKE the shades of which he had spoken, and Mademoiselle and I were left staring at the black rectangle of the broken door. I drew a deep breath and looked about me quickly. It seemed somehow as though a spell were broken, as though the curtain had lowered on some final act in the theatre. Slowly my mind seemed to free itself from a hundred illusions, and to move along more logical paths. Brutus went to the arms rack in the corner, and selected a rusted cutlass from the small arms that still rested there, thrust it at me playfully and grinned. For a minute or even more, the single log that was still burning in the fireplace hissed drowsily, and I could hear the vines tapping gently on the windows. Then I heard a pistol shot, followed by a hoarse cry. Mademoiselle started to her feet, and then sank back in her chair again, and from where I was standing I could see that her face was white and her hands were trembling. So she loved him. My hand gripped hard against the back of a chair. Why should I have hoped she did not?

"God!" she gasped. "I have killed him!"

"You?" I cried, but she did not answer.

"Huh!" said Brutus, and his grin grew broader. "Monsieur's pistol. He kill him."

"Indeed," I said, for the sense of unreality was still strong upon me. "And whom did he kill, Brutus?"

Brutus cocked his head to one side, and listened. Somewhere behind came a confusion of shouts and the thudding of horses' hoofs.

"He kill Mr. Jason Hill," said Brutus.

"Are you sure?" Mademoiselle demanded sharply.

Brutus nodded, and the dull, fixed look went out of her eyes, and slowly a touch of color returned to her cheeks.

And then there was a clamor of voices and a tramp of feet and a crash on the door outside.

Brutus looked about him in wild indecision.

"We have callers," I observed, doing my best to keep my voice calm. "Who are they, Brutus?"

Brutus, however, had forgotten me, and had sprung into the hall. At almost the same instant, someone must have discovered that the door was unlocked, for a sudden draught eddied through the passage. Then there was a confused babel of voices, to which I did not listen. I was busy swinging up the sash of the nearest window.

"Quickly, Mademoiselle!" I whispered.

"Damn it!" someone shouted from the hall. "There's another of 'em!" And there came the crack of a pistol that echoed loudly in the passage.

"It is time we were going," I said. "Out of the window, Mademoiselle!"

In my haste I almost pushed her from the sill to the lawn, and was leaning towards her.

"Mademoiselle, listen! The stables are straight to the left. Can you saddle a horse?"

She nodded.

"The first stall to the right. I shall be there in an instant!" For I remembered my sword, and sprang back into the room to get it.

"Get that man!" someone was shouting. "In after him, you fools! Don't shoot in the dark!"

I had a glimpse of Brutus darting through the passage and making a leap for the stairs. Then there was a crash of glass.

"Begad!" came a hoarse voice. "He's jumped clean through the window!" And another pistol exploded from the landing above me.

"Five hundred dollars for the man who gets him." I could swear I had heard the voice before. "Damn it! Don't let him go! Out the door, all of you! Out the door, men! Out the door!"

There was a rush of feet through the passage. I had a glimpse of men running past, and then I was half out the window.

"Stop!" someone shouted. I took a hasty glance behind me to find that my Uncle Jason had entered the morning room, his clothing torn and disarranged, the good nature erased from his face, and a gash on his left cheek that still was bleeding.

"Stop!" he shouted again, "or I fire!"

Then I was out on the lawn with the cool air from the river on my face, and running for the stable. I wonder what would have happened if the evening had been less far advanced, or the sky less overcast, or Mademoiselle less adroit than providence had made her. She had bridled the horse and was swinging the saddle on him when I had reached the stable's shadow. I could hear my uncle shouting for assistance as I tightened the girths, but Brutus must have led his men a pretty chase.

I mounted unmolested, as I somehow knew I should, and helped her up behind me. Somehow with that first crash on our front door, I knew that the game had turned. I knew that nothing would stop me. An odd sense of exaltation came over me, and with it a strange desire to laugh. It would be amusing enough when I met my father, but I wondered—I wondered as I clapped my heels into my horse's flanks.

What had my uncle to do in this affair?

CHAPTER XIV

IT WAS JUST THAT time in an autumn day when the light is fading out of the sky. The thick, heavy mists that the cold air encourages were rolling in chill and heavy from the river and leveling the hollow places in the land. The clouds were still a claret colored purple in the west, but in another few minutes that color would be gone. The shapes around us were fast losing their distinctiveness, and their outlines were becoming more and more a matter for the memory, and not the eye. And it seems to me that I never knew the air to seem more fresh and sweet.

We had broken into a sharp gallop down the rutted lane. The house, gaunt and spectral, and bleaker and more forbidding than the darkening sky, was behind us, and ahead were the broad level meadows, checkered with little clumps of willow and cedars, as meadows are that lie near the salt marshes. I had feared we might be intercepted at our gate, but I was mistaken. We had swerved to the left and were thudding down the level road, when an exclamation from Mademoiselle made me turn in my saddle. My look must have been a somewhat blank interrogation, for Mademoiselle was laughing.

"To think," she cried, "I should have said you resembled your mother! Where are we going, Monsieur?"

But I think she knew without my answering, for she laughed again, and I did not entirely blame her. It was pleasant enough to leave our house behind. It was pleasant to feel the bite of the salt wind, and to see the trees and the rocks by the roadside slip past us, gaunt and spectral in the evening. I knew the road well enough, which was fortunate, even when we turned off the beaten track over a trail which was hardly as good as a foot path. I was forced to reduce our pace to a walk, but I was confident that it did not make much difference. Once on the path, the farm was not half a mile distant, just behind a ridge of rocks that was studded by a stunted undergrowth of wind beaten oak. I knew the place. I could already picture the gaping black windows, the broken, sagging ridge pole, and the crumbling chimney. For years the wind had blown sighing through its deserted rooms, while the rain rotted the planking. It was not strange that its owners had left it, for I can imagine no more mournful or desolate spot. Our own house, three miles away, was its nearest neighbor, and scarcely a congenial one. Around it was nothing but rain sogged meadows that scarcely rose above the salt marshes that ran to the dunes where the Atlantic was beating.

As I stared grimly ahead, I could picture her there behind me, the wind whipping the color to her cheeks and playing with her hair, her eyes bright and gay in the half-light. Save for the steady plodding of the horse, it was very still. I fancied that she had leaned nearer, that her shoulder was touching mine, that I could feel her breath on my cheek. Then she spoke, and her voice was almost a whisper.

"It was good of you to take me with you," she said.

"Surely, Mademoiselle," I replied, "You did not think that I would leave you?"

"I should, if I had been you," she answered, "I was rude to you, Monsieur, and unjust to you this morning. You see I did not know."

"You did not know?"

"That the son would be as brave and as resourceful as the father. You are, Monsieur, and yet you are different."

"Yes," I said.

"And I am glad, glad," said Mademoiselle.

"And I am sorry you are glad," I said.

"You are sorry?"

"Perhaps, Mademoiselle," I replied with a tinge of bitterness I could not suppress, "if I had seen more of the world, if my clothes were in better taste, and my manners less abrupt—you would feel differently. I wonder. But let us be silent, for we are almost there."

As we drew near, making our way through damp thickets, a sense of uneasiness came over me. Somehow I feared we might be too late, though I knew that this was hardly possible. I feared, and yet I knew well enough it was written somewhere that we should meet once more. With six men after him he would not have ridden straight to the place. We should meet, and it would be different from our other meetings. I wished that it was light enough to see his face.

At a turn of the path I reined up and listened. It was very still. Already the light had gone out of the sky, and little was left of the land about us, save varying tones of black. Had he gone?

I cautiously dismounted. In a minute we should see. In a minute—Then Mademoiselle interrupted me, and I was both astonished and irritated, for my nerves were more on edge than I cared to have them. She was right. She was never overwrought.

"We are there?" she inquired.

"Softly, Mademoiselle," I cautioned her. "If you will dismount, you can see the place. It is not three hundred feet beyond the thicket. So! You will admit it is not much to look at. If you will hold the horse's head, I will go forward."

I did not listen to an objection that she was framing, but slipped hastily through the trees. As the ugly mass of the house took a more certain shape before me, I felt my pulse beat more rapidly, and not entirely through elation. Even today when I look at a place that men have built and then abandoned, something of the same feeling comes over me, but not as strongly as it did that evening. It was another matter that made me hesitate. From the shadow of the doorway I heard a sound which was too much like the raising of a pistol hammer not to make me remember that a sword was all I carried.

"There is no need to cock that pistol," I said, in a tone which I hoped sounded more confident than my state of mind. I halted, but there was no answer and no further sound.

"I said," I repeated, raising my voice, "there is no need to cock that pistol. It is a friend of Captain Shelton who is speaking."

"So," said a voice in careful, precise English. "Walk three paces forward, if you please, and slowly, v-e-r-y slowly. Now. You are a friend of the captain?"

"In a sense," I replied. "I am his son. I have come to you with a message."

"So," said the voice again, and I saw that a man was seated before me on the stone that had served as a doorstep, a man who was balancing a pistol in the palm of his hand.

"I fear I have been rude," he said, "but I find this place—what shall I say?—annoying. Your voices are alike, and I know he has a son. You say you bring a message?"

I had thought what to say.

"It is about the paper," I began. "The captain was to bring it to you here, and now he finds he cannot."

"Cannot?" he said, with the rising inflection of another language than ours. "Cannot?"

"Rather," I corrected myself hastily, "he finds it more expedient to meet you elsewhere."

"Ah," he said, "that is better. For a moment I feared the captain was dead. So the paper—he still has it?"

"He not only has it," I said, "but he is ready to give it to you—at another place he has named. You are a stranger to the country here?"

My question was not a welcome one.

"Absolute!" he replied with conviction. "Do you take me for a native of these sink holes? Mon Dieu! Does your mud so completely cover me? But surely it must be this cursed darkness, or you would have said differently. Where is this other place?"

I was glad it was too dark for him to see my smile.

"Unfortunately I cannot guide you there," I said, "for I am to stop here in case I am followed. We have had to be careful, very careful indeed—you understand?"

Impatiently he shifted his position.

"For six months," he replied irritably, "I have been doing nothing else—careful—always careful. It becomes unbearable, but where is this place you speak of—in some other bog?"

I pointed to the left of the trees where Mademoiselle was standing.

"I quite understand," I said politely, "even a day with this paper is quite enough, but it is not a bog and you can reach it quite easily. You see where I point? Simply follow that field in that direction for half a mile, perhaps, and you will come to a road. Turn to your right, and after three miles you will see a house, the first house you will meet, in fact. It has a gambrel roof and overlooks the river. Simply knock on the door so—one knock, a pause, and three in succession. It will be understood. You have a horse?"

"What is left of him," he replied, "though the good God knows how he has carried me along this far. Yes, he is attached to a post. Well, we are off, and may the paper stay still till we get it. You wait here?"

"In case we are followed," I said.

He pointed straight before him.

"I have been hearing noises over there, breaking of branches and shouts."

"Then in the name of heaven ride on," I said, and added as an afterthought, "and turn out to the side if you see anyone coming."

The pleasure I took in seeing him leave was not entirely unalloyed. As I walked to the oak thicket where Mademoiselle was waiting, I even had some vague idea of calling him back, for I do not believe in doing anyone a turn that is worse than necessary. Yet there was only one other way I could think of to keep him silent, besides sending him where he was going. She was feeding the horse handfuls of grass.

"It is quite all right, Mademoiselle," I said. "Let us move to the house. It may be more comfortable in the doorway."

We stood silently for a while, listening to the wind and the dull monotonous roar of the surf, while the night grew blacker. I listened attentively, but there was no sound. Surely he was coming.

"Tell me, Monsieur," said Mademoiselle, "what sort of woman was your mother?"

Unbidden, a picture of her came before me, that seemed strangely out of place.

"She was very beautiful," I said.

She sighed.

"And very proud," said Mademoiselle.

"Yes, very proud. Why did she call him a thief, Monsieur?"

But I did not answer.

"You are certain your father is coming?" she asked finally.

"I think there is no doubt," I told her. "I have seen him ride, Mademoiselle. It would take more than a dozen men to lay hands on him. They should have known better than let him leave the house. Listen, Mademoiselle! I believe you can hear him now."

My ears were quicker in those days. For a minute we listened in silence, and then on the wind I heard more distinctly still the regular thud of a galloping horse. So he was coming, as I knew he would. I knew he would be methodical and accurate.

"Yes, Mademoiselle," I continued, "my father has many accomplishments, but this time even he may be surprised. Who knows, Mademoiselle? Pray step back inside the doorway until I call you."

But she did not move.

"No," said Mademoiselle, "I prefer to stay where I am. I have seen too much of you and your father to leave you alone together."

"But surely, Mademoiselle," I protested, "you forget why we have come."

"Yes," she answered quickly, "yes, you are right. I do forget. I have seen too much of this, too much of utter useless folly—too many men dying, too many suffering for a hopeless cause. I have seen three men lying dead in our hall, and as many more wounded. I have seen a strong man turned into a black-guard. I have seen a son turned against his father, and all for a bit of paper which should never have been written. I hate it—do you hear me?—and if I forget it, it is because I choose. I forget it because—" She seemed about to tell me more, and then to think better of it. "Surely you see, surely you see you cannot. He is your father, Monsieur, the man who is coming here."

"Mademoiselle," I replied, "you are far too kind. I hardly think he or I have much reason to hold our lives of any particular value, but as you have said, my father was a gentleman once, and gentlemen very seldom kill their sons, nor gentlemen's sons their fathers. Pray rest assured, Mademoiselle, it will be a quiet interview. I beg you, be silent, for he is almost here."

I was not mistaken. A horse was on the path we followed, running hard, and crashing recklessly through the bushes. Before I had sight of him I heard my father's voice.

"Ives!" he called sharply. "Where the devil are you?"

And in an instant he was at the door, his horse breathing in hard, sobbing breaths, and he had swung from the saddle as I went forward to meet him.

"Here," he said, "take it, and be off. Those fools have run me over half the state. In fact," he continued in the calm tones I remember best, "in fact, I have seldom had a more interesting evening. I was fired on before I had passed the gate, and chased as though I carried the treasures of the Raj. I have your word never to tell where you got it. Never mind my reasons, or the thanks either. Take it Ives. It has saved me so many a dull day that it has quite repaid my trouble."

There he was, half a pace away, and yet he did not know me. I think it was that, more than anything else, which robbed me of my elation. To him the whole thing seemed an ordinary piece of business. I saw him test his girth, preparatory to mounting again, saw him slowly readjust his cloak, and then I took the paper he handed me and buttoned it carefully in my inside pocket. He turned to his horse again and laid a hand on his withers, but still he did not mount. I think he was staring into the night before him and listening, as I had been. Then he turned again slowly, and half faced me. On the wind, far off still, but nevertheless distinct, was the sound of voices.

"It is time we were going," said my father. "I only gave them the slip five minutes back. It was closer work than I had expected."

And then he started, and looked at me more intently through the darkness.

"Name of the devil!" said my father. "How did you get here?"

But that was all. He never even started. His hand still rested tranquilly on the reins and he still half faced me. Had it been so on that other night long ago, when his world crumbled to ruins about him? Did he always win and lose with the same passive acquiescence? Did nothing ever astonish him? There was a moment's silence, and I felt his eyes on me, and suddenly became very cautious. I knew well enough he would not let it finish in such a manner, but what could he do? The game was in my hands.

"Quite simply," I told him. "My horse was in the stable."

When he spoke again his voice was still pleasantly conversational.

"And Brutus?" he asked. "Where the devil was Brutus? Surely the age of miracles is past. Or do I see before me—" he bowed with all his old courtesy—"another David?"

"Brutus," I replied, "jumped through a second story window."

"Indeed?" he said. "He always was most agile."

"He was," I replied. "Not five minutes after you left, Uncle Jason arrived."

My father removed his hand from the reins and looped them through his arm.

"Indeed?" he said. "He came in heels first, I trust?"

"No," I said, "he is alive and well."

"The devil!" said my father, and sighed. "I am growing old, my son. I know my horse spoiled my aim, and yet he fell, and I rode over him. I had hoped to be finished with your Uncle Jason. You say he entered the house?"

"And told me to stop," I said.

"And you did not?"

"No," I replied. "I succeeded in getting out of a window also."

And then, although I could not see him, I knew he had undergone a change, and I knew that I was facing a different man.

His hand fell on my shoulder, and to my surprise, it was trembling.

"God!" he cried, in a voice that was suddenly harsh and forbidding. "Do you mean to tell me you left Mademoiselle, and never struck a blow? You left her there?"

"Not entirely," I replied.

My father became very gentle.

"Will you be done with this?" he said, "The lady, where is she now?"

And then, half to himself he added.

"How was I to know they would break in the house after I had gone?"

"Mademoiselle," I replied, "is not fifteen feet away."

His hand went up to the clasp of his cloak, and again his voice became pleasantly conversational.

"Ah, that is better," said my father. "And so you got the paper after all. Yes, I am growing old, my son. I appear to have bungled badly. Do you hope to keep the paper?"

In the distance I heard a voice again, raised in a shout. Surely he understood.

"They are coming," I said. "Yes, I intend to keep the paper."

"Indeed?" said my father. "Perhaps you will explain how, my son. I have had an active evening, but you—I confess you go quite ahead of me."

"Because," I said, "you are not anxious to go back to France, father, and you are almost on your way there."

"No, not to France," he answered, and I knew he saw my meaning.

"And yet they are coming to take you. If you so much as offer to touch me again, I shall call them, father, and we shall go back together. Your horse is tired. He cannot go much further."

He was silent for a moment, and I prudently stepped back.

"You might shoot me, of course," I added, "but a pistol shot would be equally good. Listen! I can hear them on the road."

But oddly enough, he was not disturbed.

"On the road, to be sure," said my father. "You are right, Henry, you may keep the paper. But tell me one thing more. Was there no one here when you arrived?"

"There was," I said, "but I sent him away—to our house, father."

He sighed and smoothed his cloak thoughtfully.

"I fear that I have become quite hopeless. As you say, if I fire a pistol, they will come, and now I can hardly see any reason to keep them away. So you sent him to the house, my son? And Jason is still alive? And you have got the paper? Can it be that I have failed in everything? Strange how the cards fall even if we stack the deck. Ah, well, then it is the pistols after all."

There was a blinding flash and the roar of a weapon close beside me, and I heard Mademoiselle scream. My father turned to quiet his horse.

"Do not be alarmed, Mademoiselle," he said gently, "we are not killing each other. I am merely using a somewhat rigorous method of bringing my son to his senses."

He paused, reached under his cloak, drew a second pistol and fired again. From the road there came a sound that seemed to ring pleasantly to my father's ears.

"Nearer than I thought," he said brightly. "They should be here in three minutes at the outside. Shall we sit a while and talk, my son? It is gloomy here, I admit, but still, it has its advantages. They thought my rendezvous was ten miles to the north. Lord, what fools they were! Lawton bit at the letter I let him seize as though it were pork. Ah, if it had not been for Jason! Well, everything must have an ending."

He threw his bridle over his arm, and was walking toward the doorstep, lightly buoyant, as though some weight were lifted from his mind. Hastily I seized his arm.

"Stop!" I cried. "What is to become of Mademoiselle? We cannot leave her here like this. Have you forgotten she is with us?"

Seemingly still unhurried, he paused, and glanced toward the road, and then back at me, and then for the first time he laughed, and his laughter, genuine and care-free, gave me a start which the sound of his pistol had not. The incongruity of it set my nerves on edge. Was there nothing that would give him genuine concern?

"Good God, sir!" I shouted furiously. "There's nothing to laugh about! Don't you hear them coming?"

"Ah," said my father, "I thought that would fetch you. So you have come to your senses then, and we can go on together? Untie your horse, Henry, while I charge the pistols."

My hand was on the bridle rein, when a shout close by us made me loosen the knot more quickly than I intended. I could make out the black form of a horseman moving towards us at full gallop.

"It must be Lawton," observed my father evenly. "He is well mounted, and quite reckless. I suppose we had better be going. I shall help Mademoiselle, if she will permit. No, it is not Lawton. I am sorry."

He raised his arm and fired. My horse started at the sound of his shot, and as I tried to quiet him, I saw my father lift Mademoiselle to the saddle.

"Yes," he said again, "I think it is time to be going. These men seem to have a most commendable determination. Ha! There are two more of them. Put your horse to the gallop, my son. The tide is out, and we can manage the marsh."

"The marsh!" I exclaimed.

"Quite," he replied tranquilly. "If Brutus is alive, he will have a boat near the dunes opposite. It seems as though we might be obliged to take an ocean voyage."

It seemed to me he had gone quite mad. The marsh, he knew as well as I, was as full of holes as a piece of cheese. Even in the daytime one could hardly ride across it. And then I knew that what he said was true, that he would stop at nothing; and suddenly a fear came over me. For the first time I feared the quiet, pleasant man who rode beside my bridle rein, as though we were traversing the main street of our town.

"Ah," said my father, "it is pleasant to have a little exercise. Give him the spurs Henry. We shall either get across or we shall not. There is no use being cautious."

I put my horse over a ditch, and straight ahead, I may have ridden four hundred yards with the even beating of his horse behind me, before what I feared happened. My horse stumbled, and the pull of my bridle barely got him up again. I gave him the spur, but he was failing. In a quarter of a minute he had fallen again, and this time the bridle did not raise him. I sprang free of him before he had entirely slipped down in the soft sea mud. He was lashing about desperately, nor could I get him to answer when I pulled at the bridle. My father reined up beside me and dismounted.

"His leg is broken," he said. "It is inopportune. Ah, they are still after us." And he turned to look behind him.

"Why are you waiting?" I cried. "Ride on, sir!"

"And leave you here with the paper in your pocket?" said my father. "The fall has quite got the better of you. The other pistol, Mademoiselle, if you have finished loading it. Here they come, to be sure. Would you not think the fools would realize I can hit them?"

He fired into the darkness and a riderless horse ran almost on top of us. With a snort of fright, he reared and wheeled, and a second shot answered my father's.

"Ah," said my father, "they always will shoot before they can see. The pistol from the holster, if you please, Mademoiselle."

They had not realized we had halted, for the last rider charged past us before he could check himself. I had a glimpse of his face, white against the night, and I saw him tug furiously at his bit—an unfortunate matter, so it happened, for the footing beneath the marsh grass was bad, and his horse slewed and fell on top of him.

"Pah!" exclaimed my father. "It is almost sad to watch them. Let us go, Henry. He is knocked even more senseless than he was before. Keep the saddle, Mademoiselle, and we will lead you across. I fancy that is the last of them for a moment."

So we tumbled through the mud at a walk, slipping noisily at every step, but my father was correct in his prophecy. Only the noise of our progress interrupted us. The sand dunes were becoming something more than a shadow. My father walked in tranquil silence at the bridle, while I trudged beside him.

"Are you hurt, Captain?" Mademoiselle demanded.

"Indeed not," he replied. "What was there to hurt me? I was thinking. That is all; but why do you ask, my lady?"

"Only," said Mademoiselle, "because you have been silent for the past five minutes, and you never are more gay than when you embark on an adventure. I never heard you say two words, Captain, until that night on the Loire."

"Let us forget the Loire," replied my father. "Shall I be quite frank with you, Mademoiselle?"

"It would be amusing," she admitted, leaning from the saddle towards him, "if it were only possible," she added.

"Then listen, Mademoiselle," he continued, "and I shall be very frank indeed. It must be the sea air which makes me so. I seldom talk unless I feel that my days for talking are nearly over, and at present they seem to stretch before me most interminably. In a moment we shall see the boat, and in a moment the *Sea Tern*. I fear I have been very foolish."

"Father," I inquired, "will you answer me a question?"

"Perhaps," said my father.

"What has my uncle to do with the paper?"

"My son," said my father, "may I ask you a question?"

"Perhaps," I replied.

"How much money did your mother leave you at her death?"

"She had none to leave," I replied quickly.

"Ah," said my father, "have you ever wondered why?"

"You should be able to tell me," I answered coldly.

"Indeed," said my father. "But here we are at the dunes. The boat, my son, do you see it?"

I scrambled up ahead through the sand and beach grass, and the white line of the beach, which even the darkest night can never hide, lay clear before me. A high surf was running, and beyond it I could see three lights, blinking fitfully in the black and nearer on the white sand was the shadow of a fishing boat, pulled just above the tide mark. A minute later Brutus came running toward us.

My father was evidently used to such small matters. Indeed, the whole affair seemed such a part of his daily life as to demand nothing unusual. He glanced casually at the waves and the boat, tossed off his cloak on the sand, carefully wrapped his pistols inside it, and placed the bundle carefully beneath a thwart.

"The rocket, Brutus," said my father. "If you will get in, Mademoiselle, we will contrive to push you through the breakers. Best take your coat off, my son, and place it over the pistols."

CHAPTER XV

BRUTUS HAD EVIDENTLY KEPT a slow match burning, for with a sudden flare a rocket flashed into the wind. In the momentary glare of the light I could see my father, his lips pressed together more tightly than usual, but alertly courteous as ever, helping Mademoiselle over the side, and there was Brutus grinning at me. Then the light died, and my father continued giving his directions.

"Stand by Master Henry at the stern, Brutus. I shall stay here amidships. Now into the water when I give the word. Pray do not be alarmed, Mademoiselle. There is quite nothing to bother."

A breaker crashed down on the beach ahead of us.

"Now!" he shouted, and a moment later we were up to our waists in water that was stinging in its coldness.

"Get aboard," said my father. "The oars, Brutus."

Drenched and gasping, I pulled myself over the side just as we topped a second wave. My father was beside me, as bland and unconcerned as ever.

"You see, Mademoiselle," he said, "we are quite safe. The *Sea Tern* is standing in already. While Brutus is rowing, my son, we had better load the pistols."

"Surely we are through with them," I said. The boat was tossing wildly, and Brutus was using all his strength and skill to keep it in the wind.

"Still," said my father, kneeling on the grating beside me, "let us load them. Look, Henry, I think we got off in very good time."

A knot of horsemen were galloping down the beach we had just quitted.

"They must have taken the old wagon road," he said. "I had thought as much. It becomes almost tiresome, this running away."

He reached for his cloak, placed it over Mademoiselle's shoulders, and seated himself in the stern beside her, apparently forgetful that he was drenched from head to foot.

"You are not afraid, Mademoiselle?" he asked.

"Afraid? Indeed not," I heard her reply, in a voice that was muffled by the wind. "It is a luxury, Captain, which you have made me do without too long."

"Good," said my father, a motionless shadow beside her. "If you cannot trust yourself, there are plenty of other things to trust in—God, for example, or the devil, if you prefer, or even in circumstances. How useless it is to be afraid when you remember these! Put the boat up a little more, Brutus."

And he sat silent, watching the lights of the ship towards which we were moving with each tug that Brutus gave the oars. The ship also was drawing nearer. We could make out the spars under shortened sail, and soon we were hailed from the deck. My father called back, and then there came the snapping of canvass as they put up the helm and the ship lost way tossing in the wind.

Wet and shivering, I watched her draw toward us. So this was the end after all, and I was glad it was over—glad that I would soon be quiet and alone with my thoughts. Could it have been only yesterday that I had turned my horse and passed between the sagging posts that marked the entrance to his house? Was it only a day ago I had first seen him leaning back idly in his arm chair by the fire?

My father leaned forward and thrust something into my hand.

"A pistol, Henry," he said. "Put it inside your shirt. It will be a souvenir for you when you are home again."

We could hear the waves slapping against the vessel's sides, and the orders from the deck above us. As I looked, it seemed a perilous distance away.

"Alongside, Brutus," said my father.

Two lanterns cast a feeble glow on the sheets of water that rolled under us, shouldering our frail boat impatiently in their haste to move along. Brutus pulled an oar sharply. I saw a ladder dangling perilously from the bulwarks. I saw Brutus seize it, and then our boat, arrested and stationary, began to toss madly in ill-concerted effort. My father sprang up, balancing himself lightly and accurately against each sudden roll.

"Now, Mademoiselle," he said, "we will get on deck. Brutus will carry you up quite safely. Hold the ladder, Henry, hold to it, or we may be in the water again."

His voice was still coldly precise, not raised even to a higher pitch.

"You are chilled, my son?" he asked. "Never mind, we will have brandy in a moment."

Strange how the years make the path seem smooth and mellow. As I look back on it today, boarding the ship seems a light enough matter, though I know now that every moment we remained by the ladder, eternity was staring us in the face. Even now, when I look back on it, the water is not what I see, nor Brutus grasping at the dangling rope, but rather my father, standing watching the ladder, detached from the motion and excitement around him, a passive onlooker to whom what might happen seemed a matter of small concern. Brutus, holding Mademoiselle on one arm, managed the ladder with ready adroitness, and I followed safely, but not before I had been hurled against the side with a force that nearly drove away my breath. I reached the deck to find a lantern thrust into my face, and stared into it, for the moment quite blinded.

"It is the son," remarked a voice which I thought I remembered, and then my father followed me.

"We are on board, Mr. Aiken," he called. "Never mind the boat. Get your men on the braces, or we'll blow on shore."

"Yes, Captain Shelton," said the voice again. "You are on board, to be sure, and very prettily done. I have been waiting for you all evening.

"Indeed," said my father, in his old level tone, "and who the devil are you?"

"Mr. Sims, Captain," came the reply. "I managed to seize your ship before it left the river. It is hard, after so much trouble, but you are my prisoner, Captain Shelton."

My eyes had become accustomed to the light. I looked about me to find we were in the center of a group of men. Mr. Sims, small and watchful, his face a pale yellow in the glow, was standing beside a tall man who held the lantern at arm's length. My father was facing him about two paces distant, his hand on the wet and bedraggled lapel of his coat, his glance vague and thoughtful, as though he was examining at his leisure some phenomenon of nature. Brutus, looking as unpleasant as I had ever seen him, had half thrust Mademoiselle behind his back, and stood half crouching, his eye on my father's hand, his thick lips moving nervously. My father patted his coat gently and sighed.

"I must admit," he said, "that this is surprisingly, indeed, quite delightfully unexpected. I hope you have been quite comfortable."

Mr. Sims permitted himself to smile.

"I told them you were a man of sense," he said. "Is it not odd that only you and I should have imagination and ingenuity? I knew you would see when the game is over. My compliments, Captain Shelton. You deserve to have done better."

"Of course," said my father, with a slow nod of assent, "I see when the game is over."

"I knew you would be reasonable," said Mr. Sims. "When it is finished, you and I stop playing, do we not? I am sorry we were not on the same side, but I have been commissioned to take you, captain, for a little man whom you and I both knew back in Paris. I have a dozen men aboard now, who will get us to the harbor. You are a prisoner of France, as you have doubtless guessed. We shall all be trans-shipped to Mr. Jason Hill's schooner, which has been waiting for you; and now you may go below."

Still staring thoughtfully before him, my father rested his chin in the palm of his hand.

"I remember you now," he said. "And may I add it is a pleasure to have met you? It is still a pleasure, much as I resent being taken on board a ship I own."

Mr. Sims bowed ironically.

"And now, Captain, the document, if you please, unless you care to be searched."

I thought my father had not heard, for he still looked quite blandly at the lantern.

"Would you mind telling me," he inquired, "what became of my crew? You bribed them, I suppose."

"There was only an anchor watch on deck when we came on board," said Mr. Sims. "We drove them below quite easily. The only man who gave us any trouble was your master. We had to hit him over the head when he reached the deck."

My father nodded slowly, seemed to lose his balance on the rolling deck, recovered himself, and set his feet a trifle wider apart.

"I am sincerely sorry for you, Mr. Sims," he said.

But if Mr. Sims ever asked why, it was in another life than ours. I recall his sudden bewilderment, but I never have understood exactly how it happened. I remember Brutus' eyes on my father's hand, as it moved so gently over his coat. It must have been some gesture, smooth and imperceptible. For suddenly, my father's languor left him, suddenly his lips curled back in a smile devoid of humor, and he leapt at the lantern. He leapt, and at the same instant, as perfectly timed as though the whole matter had been carefully rehearsed, Brutus' great bulk had streaked across the deck, crashing towards Mr. Sims like an unleashed fury. The speed of it, the unexpectedness, the sheer audacity, held the men around us motionless. Mr. Sims had barely time to level the pistol he was holding; but when he fired the deck was in darkness.

"This way, Mademoiselle," came my father's voice, and I ran towards it. "Hold them off, Brutus," he was calling. "Ha! It is you, my son."

While he was speaking, he darted lightly aft, and I followed. Behind me came the confused babel of struggling men. Someone was calling for a light, and someone was shrieking for help. A man with a lantern was running forward. I tripped him and we fell together, and then I felt a hand on my collar. It dragged me to my feet. I struck at it blindly, while I felt myself being half pulled, half carried through the black. And then I heard my father's voice again, close beside me, as slow and cold as ever.

"Close the door, Brutus," he said. "Listen to them. They must think we are still there."

And then I knew what had happened. Brutus had dragged me with him, and we were in a cabin. I heard my father fumbling about in the dark.

"Ah," he said, "here is the powder. Load these pistols, Brutus. Gently, you fool! Do you want to kill me?"

"You are hurt, captain," cried Mademoiselle.

"It is not worth troubling over," said my father. "And you, my lady, you are quite all right? I fear I handled you roughly. I was afraid for a moment we might be inconvenienced."

"And now," I said sarcastically, speaking into the darkness before me, "I suppose our troubles are over."

"I think so," replied my father. "Now that Brutus has thrown Mr. Sims overboard. It might be different if he were still with us. He seemed to be a determined and resourceful man. We are in the after cabin, Henry, quite the pleasantest one on the ship, and not ten paces from the wheel."

Still out of breath, still confused, I tried to look, but could see nothing. I could only smell the pungent odor of tarred rope and stale tobacco smoke. Having finished speaking, I could hear my father still moving about deliberately and moderately, seemingly well pleased at the place where we had been driven.

"Yes," he said again, "not ten paces from the wheel, and now we will finish it."

"Will you never be serious, sir?" I cried. "Do you suppose they are going to let you take charge of the ship?"

"I think so," replied my father. "But first, I must take a swallow from my flask. There is nothing like a drink to rest one. Open the port by the door, Brutus."

And I felt him groping his way past me.

"Brutus," he said, "pass the flask to my son, and give me a pistol, and steady me with your arm—so. Ah, that is better—much better...."

He fired, and the sound of his pistol in the closed room made my ears ring, and then the ship lurched, so that I had nearly lost my balance. We were rolling heavily, in the trough of the sea, and outside the canvas was snapping like a dozen small arms, and then I knew what had happened. My father had shot the man at the helm—shot him where he stood, so that the wheel had broken from his grasp, so that the ship was out of control, and the wind was blowing it on shore. Had he thought of the plan while he was watching Mr. Sims in the light of the lantern? I half suspected that he had not, but I never knew.

"Open the door, Brutus," said my father, and suddenly his voice was raised to a shout that rose above the wind and the sails.

"Keep clear of that wheel! If a single man touches it—do you hear me?—Stand clear!" And he fired again, and the *Sea Tern* still lurched in the trough of the sea.

I ran to the door beside him. Ten paces away the light of the binnacle was burning, and by it I saw two men lying huddled on the deck, and the ship's wheel whirling backwards and forwards as the waves hit the rudder.

"Get the wheel!" someone was shouting frantically. "Get the wheel! She's being blown on the bar. Get the wheel!"

"Stand clear, you dogs," called my father. "We're all going on the bar together."

"Brutus," he added, "go forward and open the forecastle, and tell my men to clear the decks. If any of these fools notice you, kill them, but they won't, Brutus, they won't. Their minds are too much set on a watery grave."

The ship heeled far over on her side as another gust of wind took her. Six men were clinging to the rail to keep their balance, staring at my father with white faces, while sea after sea swept over the bulwarks. Three of them were edging toward us, when a wave caught them and sent them sprawling almost to his feet.

"Your sword, Henry," called my father. I ducked under his arm, and stepped out on the swaying deck, but they did not wait.

"Ah," said my father, "here they come. Brutus was quicker than I could have hoped."

"Aiken!" he shouted, "are you there? Put up that helm, or we'll be drowned. Put up that helm and get your men on the braces. D'you hear me? Get some way on the ship."

A hoarse voice bellowed out an order, and another answered.

"Good," said my father. "It was a nearer thing than I expected. You can hear the breakers now. Give me your arm, my son. A lantern, Brutus."

CHAPTER XVI

AND SO IT WAS over, over almost before I could grasp what had happened.

The light that Brutus was holding showed me the white walls of the cabin, with charts nailed upon them. A table was secured to the deck, with two chairs beside it. These, two lockers and a berth made up the cabin's entire furnishings. But I hardly took the time to look about me, for the sight of my father gave me a start of consternation. His blue coat, wringing wet with sea water, and still stamped with splashes of mud, was half ripped from his shoulders. A piece of lace dangled like a dirty ribbon from his neck. The powder in his hair was clotted in little streaks of white. His face was like a piece of yellow parchment. His left arm hung limp by his side, and in his right hand he still clutched an empty pistol. He tossed it carelessly to the floor, and gripped the back of the nearest chair, staring straight at Mademoiselle, who was standing opposite, his cloak still about her. Slowly he inclined his head, and when he looked up he was smiling.

"You are quite all right, my lady?" he asked anxiously. "I am sorry you have been startled. Believe me, I did not realize this little surprise would be waiting for us. It was careless of me not to have thought, very careless. Help her to a chair, Henry."

"Will you always be polite?" she cried, with a little catch in her voice. "Will you never think of yourself? You are wounded, Captain. And what are you staring at?" she cried, turning to me. "Come here, sir, and help me with his coat."

My father sank into a chair, and his pale lips relaxed.

"Pray do not concern yourself," he replied gravely. "I think of myself, Mademoiselle, of myself always, and now I am very fortunate, but the blue from my coat is running on your dress. Brutus will see to me, Mademoiselle. He is quite used to it. The rum, Brutus. You will find it in the starboard locker."

But it was Mademoiselle who found the bottle and poured him a glass. He drank it quickly.

"Again, if you please," he said, and a shade of color returned to his cheeks. "The water was uncommonly cold tonight. How much better the sea would be, if the Lord had mixed in a dash of spirits. There is a coat in the locker, Brutus, and you may find some splints and a piece of twine. I fear my arm is broken."

Mademoiselle had taken Brutus' knife and was cutting away his sleeve, half soaked with blood. He sighed and smiled a little sadly.

"So Sims hit me after all," he said. "It must be age. I was not so clumsy once. The bandages, Brutus."

He watched us with a mild interest, and then his mind turned to other matters, and he seemed regardless of the pain we caused him.

"My son," he said, turning to me, "you made a statement a while ago which interested me strangely. I was preoccupied, and perhaps I did not hear you aright, but it seemed you said I should know what had become of your mother's money. What am I to understand by that?"

"You are hurt, sir," I replied. "Why go into a painful matter now? We have kept it quiet long enough. Only three people knew that it happened, and one of them is dead. Let us forget it, father. I am willing if you are."

My father raised his eyebrows, and it seemed to me that pain had made his face look older, and not even the smile on his lips concealed little lines of suffering.

"And what are we to forget?" he asked.

"Surely you know," I said.

"No," said my father, "I do not. Out with it—what are we to forget?"

Was he still acting? Was it ever possible to understand him? Perhaps even now he was turning the situation into a jest, and smiling to himself as he watched me. And yet somehow I had ceased to hate him.

"Do you mean," I asked "that you never took it?"

Slowly my father's body straightened in his chair, and his lips, drawn tight together, seemed to repress an exclamation.

"So he told you that," he said. "He told you that I made off with her fortune? Gad! but he was clever, very, very clever."

He paused, and refilled his glass, and held it steadily before him. His voice, when he spoke, was gentle, and, like his face, strung taut with pain.

"No wonder she never sent me word," he murmured.

"Do you mean," I asked, "that you never took it?"

For a second he did not reply—only looked thoughtfully before him, as if he saw something that we would never see.

"Why go into a painful matter now?" said my father at length. "Brutus, call in Mr. Aiken."

He lurched into the cabin a half a minute later. His sea cloak was gone. His shirt, none too white the previous afternoon, was torn and scraped as though it had scrubbed the deck, and he had transferred his red handkerchief from his neck to his head, so that his tangled hair waved around it like some wild halo. His heavy hands, bruised and scarred, were working restlessly at his sides. He glanced at my father's bandaged arm, and his jaw thrust forward.

"I warned 'em, captain," he cried hoarsely. "By heaven, I warned 'em. 'Damn you,' I says, 'hell will break loose when the captain climbs aboard,' and it did, so help me. There was fifteen of 'em and now there's six, and the crew has 'em in the forecastle now, beating 'em, sir! And now, by thunder, we'll sling 'em overboard!"

"That would be a pity," said my father. "Let them sail with us. I shall make it more unpleasant than drowning. Which way are we heading, Ned?"

"Due east by south," said Mr. Aiken, "and we're ready to show heels to anything. I can drop a reef off now if you want it."

"Good," said my father. "Put on all the sail she will carry."

Mr. Aiken grinned.

"I thought you'd want to be moving," he said.

"Quite right," said my father, "and put about at once and head back up the river."

Mr. Aiken whistled softly.

"Well, I'll be damned!" he muttered.

"I shall want ten men with me when I land," my father continued. "I've done my best to keep the crew out of my private affairs, but now it seems impossible."

"They'd all like to go," said Mr. Aiken. "They've been hoping for excitement all day, sir."

"Ten will be quite enough," said my father.

"What is it you are saying?" Mademoiselle asked sharply.

"Quite nothing," he replied, "except that we are going back."

His arm must have given him a twinge, for his face had grown very white.

"Surely you have done enough," she said, and her voice became a soft entreaty. "Here we are on board your ship. If I told you I was not entirely sorry, would you not go on? If I told you, captain, I did not care about the paper——?"

My father waved his hand in graceful denial.

"Not go back? Ah, Mademoiselle," he added in grave rebuke, "can it be possible after all, in spite of all this—let us say regrettable melodrama—you are forgetting I am the villain of this piece, and not a very pleasant one? Even if I wished, my lady, my sense of hospitality would forbid it. My brother-in-law is waiting for me under my roof tonight, and I could not leave him alone. He would be disappointed, I feel sure, and so would I. I have had a strenuous evening. I need recreation now. Load the pistols, Brutus."

And he fell silent again, his eyes on the blank wall before him, his fingers playing with his glass.

The *Sea Tern* had need to be a fast ship, and she lived up to requirements. The easterly wind sent her lightly before it, cutting sheer and quick through the roughened sea. With his arm in a sling of white linen, my father sat motionless, apparently passive and regardless of the flight of time. It was only when we veered in the wind and orders were shouted from forward that he looked about him.

"Your arm, Brutus," he said.

On deck the crew was at work about the long boat, and over the port rail, perhaps a quarter of a mile away, I could see our house, with a light burning in the window, flickering through the waving branches of the elms that half hid it. Nearer lay our wharf, a black, silent shadow. My father watched without a word. The anchor chain growled out a sharp complaint, and the anchor splashed into the tide.

"Mr. Aiken," said my father, "give orders to get under way in half an hour. When we land, the men will wait at the wharf, and be ready to enter the house when you call them. You shall come with me, my son. I can still show you something amusing and instructive."

"And I?" Mademoiselle demanded. "Shall you leave me here?"

He seemed to hesitate for a moment.

"Earlier in the evening, Mademoiselle," he replied, "I had given orders for my sloop to carry you to New Orleans. Your boxes will be taken from the house, and you will be taken on board from here. May you have a pleasant journey, and may your friends be well when you arrive."

"You mean it is good-by?" she asked, and her voice had a sound that reminded me of tears. "You mean we shall not meet again?"

He bowed low over her hand.

"Mademoiselle will be relieved to know we shall not," said my father gravely. "Let me hope you may always have more pleasant company."

She seemed about to speak again, but she did not. Instead, she turned silently away and left him, and a second later I saw her disappear in the shadow of the main-mast.

"Ah," said my father, "there is a woman for you. My son, in the side pocket of my coat you will find a snuff box. Would you kindly open it for me and permit me to take a pinch? And you, perhaps? No? It is a pleasant sedative."

He took a step nearer the rail, and the men about the long boat stiffened to attention.

"Get them into the boat, Mr. Aiken," he said, "You and I will sit in the stern, my son. Your arm, Brutus, so."

"Stand by to lower away," directed Mr. Aiken in a harsh undertone; and the blocks creaked and we were in the river.

The oars had been muffled, so that we moved to the wharf in silence.

"Land the men, and tell them to wait," said my father. "You shall come with us, Mr. Aiken, and you, my son, and you, Brutus."

We walked silently up the path, with Brutus and my father in the lead. Once he paused and listened, and then proceeded forward.

"I believe," said my father, "he is quite alone. Ha!"

He had stopped dead, and Brutus had leapt forward, crashing into a dense thicket of overgrown bushes.

"Put up your pistol, Ned," said my father. "Brutus has him."

There was a moment's silence, followed by a faint cry.

"Bring him here, Brutus," said my father. The bushes cracked again, and Brutus was back.

"Now who the devil may you be?" inquired my father, striding towards the figure that Brutus was holding, and then he paused, and in the dark I fancied he was reaching for his coat lapel.

"Lunacy, thy name is woman," said my father softly. "Will they never stay where they are placed?"

It was Mademoiselle whom Brutus had thrust before him.

"I came in the boat," she stammered brokenly. "I—"

"You wanted to see the end, my lady?" my father inquired. "Surely you should have known better, but it is too late now. You are going to be present at a harrowing scene, which I hoped to save you. Mr. Aiken, help the lady over the path."

And we proceeded to the house together. A minute later we made our way over the rough, unkempt grass which once marked our brick terrace. Brutus opened the door and we were in the dark hall, lighted by a square of candle light from the morning room. He paused again and listened, and then strode across the threshold. A blaze was burning high in the morning fireplace, and six candles were lighted on the center table, and seated before it, examining my father's papers, were my Uncle Jason and Mr. Lawton.

"Ha!" cried Mr. Lawton, springing to his feet and eyeing my father intently. "So you are here, Shelton, and every card in the deck."

He paused to nod and rub his hands.

"Yes, b'gad! There's the girl and there's the boy and there's the negro. It was Sims' idea your getting on the boat. He's bright as a trap, Jason. I told you he was."

My father sighed a little sadly.

"He was indeed," he admitted.

My uncle surveyed him with his broadest smile, and his eyes twinkled with a malign amusement, that was not wholly pleasant.

"So here you are, George," he cried in a voice that seemed to shake with excitement. "God help you, but I won't or your son either, no, or the lady."

"Indeed?" inquired my father. "Pray go on, Jason. I had forgotten you were diverting, or is it one of your latest virtues."

A slight crease appeared between my uncle's eyes, and his face became a trifle redder.

"So you still are jovial," he said. "I admire you for it, George. Yes, I admire you, because of course you know what is going to happen to you, George, and to your son also. Perhaps you will wipe away that smirk of yours when a French firing squad backs you against a wall."

My father adjusted the bandage on his arm, and smiled, but his eyes had become bright and glassy.

"So you have quite decided to send me to France, Jason?" he inquired pleasantly. "Of course, I suspected it from the first. I knew you hated me, and naturally my son. I knew you never felt the same after our little falling out, when I found you forging—what am I saying?—reading the letter I sent to Mr. Aiken. Gad! but your face was pasty then, you sly dog—"

He paused and took a step toward him. He was a different man when he continued. It seemed as though some resistance in him was breaking down, as though the years of repression were falling away. A hot, dull red had come into his cheeks, and burned there like a fever. His whole body trembled, shaken by some emotion which I could not fathom. His voice grew sharp and discordant, his words hot and triumphant.

"Almost as pasty as when you challenged me to produce those damned bales of fur. Do you remember, Jason? The party here at this house—the music, the flowers? Oh, they were all there! And of course I had put the shavings on my boat. You could prove it, and you could too, Lawton, do you remember? And you could swear to it, and you could swear I had cheated you before, that I had stolen your card money. Oh, you caught me. You brought the wolf to bay and drew the sword of justice!"

Mr. Lawton half started from his seat.

"Be still, Shelton," he snapped, "or I'll have them gag you."

My father clenched his fist, drew a deep breath, and his voice lost its strident note.

"Ah, Lawton, Lawton," he said. "Will you always be impetuous? Will you never be subtle, but always crude, always the true rough diamond with the keen edge? No, you won't gag me, Lawton.

"And so you will send me to France, Jason, and my son too, criminals to justice. It is thoughtful of you to think of justice, but tell me, Jason. Is it I you hate, or my wife's money that you love? Tell me, Jason, I have often wondered."

My uncle's face also became a flaming red; the veins stood out on his temples. He tried to speak, but his words choked him.

"Sims," shouted Mr. Lawton. "Sims! Take him out! Take him away!"

My father raised his eyes to the ceiling and sighed.

"Ah Lawton," he said. "Is it possible that you did not know it? Can it be that you do not understand? Poor Sims is dead, Lawton, a brave man, but not of good physique. The evening was quite too much for him. Do not take it so hard, man! We all must die, you among the rest. You should have known me better, Lawton. You should have known I would not allow myself to be taken prisoner."

"What!" shouted Mr. Lawton. "What the devil are you then?"

The scene appeared to move my father, for he sighed again, and paused, the better to enjoy it.

"Only a poor man," he said, "only a poor chattel of the Lord's, a poor frail jug that has gone too often to the well. A poor man of a blackened reputation, who has been set upon by spies of France, and threatened in his own house, but who has managed to escape—" and his voice became sharp and hard.

"Take Mr. Lawton's pistol, Ned."

There fell a moment's silence in the room while my father, a little in advance of the rest of us, stared fixedly into my uncle's eyes.

"Set upon by spies," he said, "persecuted and driven. It has set me thinking, Jason. As I walked back here tonight, I still was thinking, and can you imagine what was on my mind? It was you, Jason, you and Lawton. And as I thought of you, my mind fell, as it naturally would, on holy things, and a piece of the Scripture came back to me. Think of it, Jason, a piece of the Holy Writ. Would you care to hear it?"

My father paused to adjust a wrinkle in his coat, and then his voice became solemn and sonorous, and he spoke the words with metrical precision.

"'To everything'," said my father, "there is a season, and a time to every purpose under the heaven. A time to be born and a time to die'."

He paused long enough to nod from one to the other.

"'A time to plant and a time to pluck up that which is planted'."

He raised his eyes to the ceiling again, and placed the tips of his fingers together.

"And 'a time to kill'," he concluded gently. His words died softly away in the quiet room.

"I have often thought of that passage," he continued. "Many and many a night I have repeated it to myself, under stars and under roof, and sometimes I have prayed, Jason. Oh yes, we all pray sometimes. Sometimes I have prayed for the time to come."

The red had gone out of my uncle's face, and Mr. Lawton was sitting rigid in his chair, his eyes glued on the slender figure before him.

"And now," said my father, in a tone that was as near to the pious as I ever heard him utter, "now it is here, and I thank thee, Lord."

"Good God!" gasped Mr. Lawton, in a voice that rose only a little above a whisper. "Do you mean to murder us?"

My father still stood motionless, but when he spoke again his voice had relapsed to its old genial courtesy.

"What a word for gentlemen to use!" he exclaimed in polite rebuke. "Murder you? Of course not, Lawton. I am simply about to propose a game. That is all, an exciting little game. Only one of us will die. Clear the large table of the papers, Ned. Toss them on the floor."

CHAPTER XVII

OF ALL THE PEOPLE in the room, my father alone retained his self-possession. My uncle's cheeks had sagged, and perspiration made them moist and shiny, and Mr. Lawton seemed bent and as wrinkled as though he had aged a dozen years.

"Brutus," said my father, "place the pistols on the table, the ones I gave you as we came on shore. Side by side, Brutus. The silver mountings look well against the dark mahogany. Do they not cheer you, Jason? And now, Brutus, a pack of cards from the bookshelves. It will be a pretty game, Lawton, as pretty a game as you have ever played."

"Good God! What are you going to do, Shelton?" stammered Mr. Lawton, and he raised a trembling hand to his forehead.

"You grow interested?" my father inquired. "I thought you would, Lawton, and now stand up and listen! And you too, Jason. Stand up, you dog! Stand up! The world is still rolling. Are you ill?"

And indeed, my uncle seemed incapable of moving.

"Perhaps you would prefer to sit," said my father politely. "I have known people who find it steadies them to fire across the table while seated in a chair. Your attention, then, and I will tell you the game. On the table are three pistols. One of them is loaded. The question is—which? They are all made by the same smith. And yet one is different. We shall find out which it is in a few minutes. Shuffle the cards, Lawton. You and Jason shall draw. The low number selects the first pistol, and is first to fire, and then the next. I shall take the last pistol, and we shall stand across the table, you and Jason where you are, while I stand over here. Brutus, give the cards to Mr. Lawton."

My father smiled and bowed. From his manner it might have been some treat he was proposing, some pleasant bit of sport that all knew ended in hilarity. Still smiling, he glanced from one to the other, and then towards Mademoiselle and me, as though seeking our approbation. Even with his bandaged arm and weather stained clothes, he carried himself with a gaiety and grace.

"Always trust in chance, my son," he said.

My uncle leaned forward, and drew his hand across his lips, his eyes blank and staring.

"And if you get the pistol?" he demanded hoarsely.

"In that case," replied my father, "Your troubles will be over, Jason. Pray rest assured—I shall attend to that. And then, when that is finished Brutus shall bring two other pistols, and Lawton and I shall draw again."

Mr. Lawton grasped the cards uncertainly.

"You give us the first two choices?" he demanded.

"The host naturally is last," said my father. "One must always be polite."

"Then you're mad," said Mr. Lawton bluntly. "Come, Shelton, step outside, and we'll finish it on the lawn."

"And I should undoubtedly kill you," said my father. "Pray do not tempt me, Lawton."

"I tell you, you're mad," said Mr. Lawton.

"I have told that once before today," said my father. "And still I am not sure. I have often pictured this little scene, Lawton. We have only one thing to add to it. Now tell me if I'm mad."

My father had reached up to his throat, and was fumbling at his collar. When he drew away his hand, something glittered between his fingers. Silently he placed his closed fist on the table, opened it, and there was the gold locket which I had perceived in the morning. He pressed the spring, and the lid flew free. Mr. Lawton leaned forward, glanced at the picture inside, and then drew back very straight and pale.

"Come, Lawton," said my father gravely. "Which is it now—madness or an appeal for justice and retribution? With her picture on the table, Lawton, I have wondered—I have often wondered, Lawton—who will be the lucky man to draw the loaded pistol? Let us leave it there, where we can watch it before we fire. I have often thought that she would like it so. And now—" he nodded again and smiled,—"surely you will oblige me. Shuffle the cards, Lawton, and let the game go on."

Mr. Lawton bit his lower lip, fingered the cards uncertainly, and then tossed them in the fire.

"Come, come, Lawton," said my father sharply. "Where are your manners? Surely you are not afraid, not afraid of a picture, Lawton?"

"No," said Mr. Lawton, "I am not afraid."

"Ah," said my father, "I thought I knew you better. Another pack of cards for Mr. Lawton, Brutus. Let us trust, Lawton, that these will suit you better."

"You misunderstand me," said Mr. Lawton simply. "I am not going to play."

"Not going to play?" exclaimed my father, raising his eyebrows.

Slowly Mr. Lawton shook his head.

"You are far too generous, Shelton," he said. "If you shot me where I stand, you would only be giving me my fair deserts. If I had been in your place and you in mine, both you and Jason would have been dead ten seconds after I had entered the door."

"Don't be a fool, Lawton," cried my father, raising his hand. "Think what you are saying!"

"I have thought," he replied sharply. "The game is over, Shelton, and I know when I am beaten. We have not got the paper, Jason, and you remember what I said. If you failed to get it, I should tell the whole story, and now, by heaven, I will. Every man in town will know it tomorrow morning. I told you I would be shut out of this business, and I mean it, Jason."

On my father's face came something closer to blank astonishment than I had ever seen there. Something in the situation was puzzling him, and for the moment he seemed unable to cope with it.

"Lawton," he said slowly, "shuffle those cards, or I'll shoot you where you stand."

Mr. Lawton placed the cards on the table, and adjusted them thoughtfully.

"No, you won't," he replied. "I know you better than that. You would never draw a weapon on any man unless he had an equal chance, and I haven't, Shelton."

I had stepped forward beside him. Was there someone else at the bottom of the whole wretched business? Was it possible that my father had no hand in it? A glance at Mr. Lawton answered a half a hundred questions which were darting through my mind.

And my father was still staring in a baffled way, eyeing Mr. Lawton in silent wonder.

"So," he said, "you think I'll forgive you? Is it possible you are relying on my Christian spirit?"

"No," said Mr. Lawton, "I do not ask you to forgive me. I am saying I have stopped. That is all—stopped, do you understand me? I should nave stopped when Jason commissioned me to kill your son. I should have, if this affair with France was not beginning. Even then the business sickened me. What did I care about the money he stole from her? I did not want her money. What did I care if the boy suspected you had not stolen it, but that Jason had it all the time? I couldn't have killed him, because he had some slight glimmerings of sense."

A dozen dim suspicions clashed suddenly together into fact. I looked sharply at my father. He was nodding, with some faint suspicion of amusement.

"And so you did not," he said gently. "Your scruples do you credit, after all."

"It was just as well," said Mr. Lawton. "I thought the news your son was attacked would fetch you over. Jason did his best to hush it up, but I knew you would suspect. And you know what it would have meant to me if I could have sent you back to France."

And yet, for some reason, my father was strangely ill at ease. Like someone detected in a falsehood, he looked restlessly about him. For the moment his adroitness seemed to have left him. He made a helpless little gesture of annoyance.

"You say you have stopped?" inquired my father. "Then why not do so, Lawton, and stop talking. Do you think what you say interests me? Do you think I do not know the whole damnable business, without your raking it up again? Why should Jason have wished to be rid of me except for her money? Why should you have helped him, except—At least it was not for money, Lawton."

But Mr. Lawton did not heed my father's voice. His glance had come to rest again upon the locket on the table, and the hard lines about his mouth had vanished.

"And she never spoke to me, never looked at me again," he said.

My father started and looked at him quickly.

"Lawton," groaned my uncle, "are you out of your mind?"

Mr. Lawton turned sharp around and faced him with a scowl.

"I told you," he said harshly. "I told you to get me the paper, and I told you what would happen if you did not, and it is happening already, Jason. I am going to tell the story."

My uncle moved convulsively to his feet, and his voice was sharp and malignant.

"Do you suppose anyone will believe you?" he cried. "Do you fancy they will take your word against mine?"

"We will try it," said Mr. Lawton. "There are still people who wonder why Shelton stooped to the thing you accused him of. We certainly will try it."

"And if you do," said my uncle, "I will show it was she who did it—that it was she who urged him on. I'll tell them! D'you hear me? I'll tell them, and they'll take my word for it. They'll take my word!"

"God!" cried Mr. Lawton. "So that's the reason! So that's the trick you played. You dog! If I had only known—"

His face had become blanched with passion, and my uncle staggered back before his upraised hand, but Mr. Lawton did not strike. For a moment he stood rigid, and when he spoke he had regained his self-control.

"You will never tell it, Jason," he said slowly, and then he turned to my father, and inclined his head very gravely, and his voice was no longer harsh and strident.

"I often wondered why you left her so," he said, "and why you did not face it. You feared her name might be dragged in the mire! Because he threatened to bring her into that miserable business, you never raised a hand. I always knew you were a gentleman, but I did not know you were Don Quixote de la Mancha."

For the first time since the two had spoken, my father moved. He leaned across the table, picked up the locket very gently, and placed it in his coat. His eyes rested on Lawton, and returned his bow.

"Rubbish!" said my father. "One liar is bad enough, but why listen to two? We will leave her name out of the conversation. Perhaps I had other reasons for going away. Did they ever occur to you, Lawton? Perhaps, for instance, I was sick of the whole business. Did you ever think I might have found it pleasant to leave so uncongenial an atmosphere, that I was relieved, delighted at the opportunity to leave lying relatives, and friends who turned their backs? Faugh! I have kept the matter quiet for fifteen years, merely because I was too indolent to stand against it. I was too glad to see the cards fall as they did to call for a new deal. There I was, tied up to a family of sniveling hypocrites. Look at Jason, look at him. Who wouldn't have been glad to get away?"

And he bowed to my uncle ironically.

"Positively, I was glad to hear the crash. 'Very well,' I said, 'I am a thief, since it pleases you to think so.' Thieves at least are a more interesting society, and I have found them so, Lawton, not only more interesting, but more honest."

But somehow there was no ring of conviction to his words. His voice seemed unable to assume its old cynicism, and his face had lost its former placidity. It had suddenly become old and careworn. Pain and regret, sharp and poignant, were reflected there. His eyes seemed strained and tired, the corners of his mouth had drooped, and his body too was less erect and resolute. Something had been broken. For a moment, his mask and his mantle had dropped where he could not find them. And then, as he stood looking ahead of him at the shadows, he ended his speech in a way that had no logic and no relation to the rest.

"If she had only said she did not believe them—Why did she not say it?"

And then he squared his shoulders and tried again to smile.

"But what difference does it make now? The road has turned too long ago for us to face about."

"She never spoke to me, never looked at me again!" repeated Mr. Lawton.

My father's fist crashed down on the table, but when he spoke his words were precise and devoid of all emotion.

"And why the devil should she," he answered. "We are not questioning her taste. And you, Jason," he added. "No one will doubt your word, or believe this little romance. Do you wonder why? They will never have the opportunity. Brutus, take them down to the boat."

Brutus stepped forward and laid a hand on my uncle's shoulder. He shrank back.

"George," he cried, "you shall have the money. I swear it, George. I have wronged you, but—"

"Yes," said my father, "I shall have the money, and you too, Jason. I shall have everything. Take them along, Brutus," and they left the room in silence, while my father watched them thoughtfully, and arranged the lapel on his coat.

"Ned," said my father, "the rum decanter is over on the bookshelves. Good God, where is he going?" for Mr. Aiken had darted into the hall, and was running up the staircase.

"Is the man mad? Is—"

My father stopped, and was looking at the table. I followed his glance, and started involuntarily. There had been three pistols lying side by side on the polished mahogany, and now there were only two.

"My son," said my father, "the rum decanter is on the bookshelves. The glasses—"

A shout from the hall interrupted him.

"B'gad, captain!" Mr. Aiken was roaring. "Damme! Here's another of 'em! You would bite me, would you! Hell's fire if I don't cut your gullet open."

"What an evening we are having, to be sure," said my father, turning to the doorway.

Mr. Aiken was pushing a man before him into the room, and holding a dirk at his throat.

"Ives!" shrieked Mademoiselle.

"She is right," said my father. "It is Ives de Blanzy. I had forgotten you had sent him to the house."

The man Mr. Aiken was holding wrenched himself free, and sprang forward, shaking a fist in my father's face.

"Forgotten!" he shouted. Was it you who sent me here and had me tied in the cellar, and left me chewing at the rope, and set this pirate on me? Mother of God! Captain Shelton! Is this a joke you are playing—"

"Only a very regrettable error," said my father. "A mistake of my son's. Pray calm yourself, Ives. It is quite all right. My son, this is Mademoiselle's brother."

"Her brother!" I cried.

"And who the devil did you think I was?" He walked slowly towards me. "Have you no perceptions?"

He would have continued further, if my father had not laid a hand on his arm.

"Gently, Ives," he said. "You know I would not treat you so. Give him the paper, my son. He is the one who should have it."

I stared at my father in blank astonishment, but before I could speak, he had continued.

"I know what you are thinking. What was the use of all this comedy? Why should I have deceived you? I was only running true to form, my son, which is the only thing left to do when life tastes bitter. Do you not understand? But you do not. Your palate is unused yet to gall and wormwood. Only wait, my son—"

He raised his hand slowly, as though tilting an imaginary glass to his lips.

"Only wait. They will offer you the cup some day, and we were always heavy drinkers. Pray God that you will stand it with a better grace than I—that you will forget the sting and rancor of it, and not carry it with you through the years."

His eyes grew brighter as he spoke, and his features were suddenly mobile and expressive.

"She said she believed it. She threw their lies in my face. She lashed me with them, and my blood was hotter then than now. She would not listen, and I forgot it was a woman's way. How was I to know it was only impulse? I ask you—how was I to know? Was I a man to crawl back, and ask her forgiveness, to offer some miserable excuse she would not credit? And you, brought into manhood to believe I was a thief—was I to stand your flinging back my denial? Was I to pose as the picture of injured innocence, and beg you the favor of believing? I would not have expected it of you, my son. By heaven, it would have stuck in my throat. I had gone my way too long, and the draught still tasted bitter. It burned, burned as I never thought it would again, when I first saw you standing watching me. Indeed it is only now that its taste has wholly gone—only now that I see what I have done, now when the lights are dim, and it is too late to begin again."

He stopped and squared his shoulders and the harshness left his voice.

"You understand, I hope," he added "Give him the paper, Henry." And he nodded towards Ives de Blanzy.

I drew it from my pocket, and handed it to him in silence.

"Now what is the meaning of this?" said Ives de Blanzy harshly. "This is not the paper! The cursed thing is blank inside!"

My father snatched it from his hands.

"Blank!" he muttered. "Blank! Clean as the driven snow! Is it possible I have failed in everything?"

Mademoiselle had moved forward, and touched his arm. He glanced at her quickly, and slowly his frown vanished.

"Naturally it is blank, captain," said Mademoiselle. "I took the real one from you this morning when you left it in your volume of Rabelais. I thought that you might place it there. I am sorry, captain, sorry now that you made me take you seriously."

The paper dropped from his fingers and fluttered to the floor, but strangely enough he did not appear chagrined. His gallantry was back with him again, and with it all his courtesy.

"Ah, Mademoiselle," he said, "I should have known you better. Will there always be a woman where there is trouble?"

"And you have not made me hate you, Captain," Mademoiselle continued.

"But you, my son," said my father, "you understand?"

I felt his glance, but I could not meet it.

"Yes," I said, "I understand."

"Good," said my father. "Here comes Brutus. And now we shall have our rum."

"I understand," I said, and my voice seemed unsteady, "that you are a very brave and upright gentleman."

"The devil!" cried my father.

And then he started and whirled toward the door.

"Ned! Ives!" he called sharply. "What the devil is going on outside?" and the three of them had darted into the hall.

Clear and distinct through the quiet night had come a shriek and the report of a pistol.

I started to follow them, but Mademoiselle had laid a hand on my arm, and was pointing to the table. I lifted first one and then the other of the two pistols that were lying there. Neither was primed. Neither was loaded.

"The third one," she said quietly, "Mr. Lawton took. No, no," she added, as I started toward the door, "Stay here, Monsieur. It is not your affair."

CHAPTER XVIII

SHE STILL STOOD LOOKING at the pistols on the table. Was she thinking, as I was, of the irony, and the comedy and the tragedy that had been so strangely blended in the last hour? Slowly she turned and faced me, her slender fingers tugging aimlessly at her handkerchief. For a moment her eyes met mine. Then she looked away, and the color had deepened in her cheeks.

"So," said Mademoiselle, "It is almost over. Are you not glad, Monsieur, that it is finished?"

The wick of a candle had dropped to the wax, and was spluttering fitfully. Mechanically I moved to fix it.

"No," I said, "I am not glad."

"Not glad? Surely you are glad it has ended so. Surely you are glad your father—"

"No," I said, and my voice was so much louder than I had intended that the sound of it in the quiet room made me stop abruptly. She looked up at me, a little startled.

"At least Monsieur is frank," she said. "Do you know—have you thought that you are the only one of us who has been wholly so, who has not had something to conceal? Pray go on, Monsieur. It is pleasant to hear someone who is frank again. Continue! You must be glad for something. Every cloud must have—do you not say—a silver lining? If it is not your father—surely you are glad about me?"

She made a graceful little gesture of interrogation.

"Come, come," she went on, "You are not yourself tonight. Never have I seen you look so black. Think, Monsieur! The men are on deck and the wind is fair. Soon I shall be going. Soon you will forget."

"No," I said, "Mademoiselle is mistaken. I shall not forget."

"Nor I," she said gravely, "I wonder, Monsieur, if you understand—but you cannot understand what it has meant to me. I have tried to tell you once before, but you are cold, like your father. I have seen many men who have said gallant things, but only you two of all I know have done them."

"I have done nothing," I said. "You know I have done nothing."

"But it has not been your fault," she answered. "And was it nothing to protect a stranger from a strange land, when you had nothing to gain from it and everything to lose?"

"Mademoiselle forgets," I said, "that I had nothing to lose. It was lost already."

"Then surely," she replied lightly, "surely you must be glad I am going?"

"You know better than that," I answered. "Ah, Mademoiselle, do you not see? I hoped I might show you that I did not always blunder. I hoped I might show you—"

The words seemed to choke me.

"Ah, Mademoiselle," I cried, "if I had only been on the stairs at Blanzy!"

"Blanzy!" she echoed, "Pray what has Blanzy to do with you and me?"

Even now I do not know what made me speak, save that she was going. The very ticking of the clock was bringing the moment nearer, and there she was, staring at me, wide-eyed, half puzzled and half frightened. It seemed already as though she were further away.

"Do you not see?" I said. "It is not like you not to understand. Nor is it very kind. How can I see you go and be glad? How can I be glad you love my father?"

"Mon Dieu!" she exclaimed suddenly startled, "Your father! I care for your father!"

I bowed in quick contrition.

"Mademoiselle," I said, "I fear I have been very rude, and, as usual, very gauche. I beg you to forgive me."

"But I tell you," she cried, "I do not love him!"

I bowed again in silence.

"You do not believe me?"

"Mademoiselle may rest assured," I replied gently, "that I understand—perfectly."

"You!" I started at her sudden vexation, started to find that her eyes were filled with tears.

"You understand quite nothing! Never have I seen anyone so cruel, so stupid!"

"Mademoiselle," I said, "I have been awkward, but forgive me—the cabin of the *Sea Tern*, where you asked him to sail on, and when you bade him recall what he said on the stairs at Blanzy.... Your pardon! I have been very blunt."

And now she was regarding me with blank astonishment.

"Surely he told you," she murmured, "Surely he told you what the Marquis had intended."

Then she stopped, confused and silent.

"Mon Dieu!" she exclaimed suddenly, "But he has told you nothing!"

"No," I said dully, "He has been most discreet. But does it make any real difference, Mademoiselle, except that I know now that the Marquis was a man of very keen discrimination?"

"Are you mad?" cried Mademoiselle, "I tell you it is not your father. I tell you I—"

Her face had grown scarlet. She bowed her head, and tugged more violently than ever at the corner of her handkerchief.

"Mademoiselle," I said unsteadily, "Mademoiselle, what was it he told you at Blanzy?"

"I cannot tell you if you do not know," she answered, "Indeed I cannot."

"But you will!" I cried. "You will, Mademoiselle! You must! Mademoiselle—"

Her eyes had met mine again.

"They were breaking in the door," she began, "and he was going down to meet them. I told him—I told him to go, to leave me, and take the paper. He said—"

She paused again, watching me in vague embarrassment.

"He said he'd be damned if he would, Monsieur. He said he would do what the Marquis had directed, if he had to swing for it. That he would take the paper and me to America—that I ... Mon Dieu! Do you not know what he said! Can you not guess?... He said that I was to marry his son."

A smile suddenly played about her lips.

"And I told him," she continued breathlessly, "I told him I'd be damned if I would, Monsieur. That neither he nor the Marquis would make me marry a man I did not know, much less a son of his!"

"And when you asked him to recall it—Mademoiselle, when you asked him to recall it, did you mean—tell me, Mademoiselle!"

"Ah," she whispered, "but it is too soon, and you are too rough, Monsieur! I beg of you—be careful! Besides—someone is coming."

And then I heard a soft footstep behind me.

"Huh!" said Brutus, "I go tell the captain. No. It is all right. I tell the captain. He is happy. It will please him. Huh!" His long speech seemed to have taken his breath, for he paused, grinning broadly.

"Huh!" he said finally. "Mr. Lawton shoot Mr. Jason. Shoot him with pistol off the table. The captain is happy."

But before Brutus could turn to go, my father was in the doorway, smoothing the bandage on his arm.

"Let us say relieved, Brutus," he answered smoothly. "It is dangerous ever to use superlatives."

Then he glanced from Mademoiselle to me, and his smile broadened.

"Very much relieved," he said, "and yet—and yet I still feel thirsty. The rum decanter, Brutus."

www.ingramcontent.com/pod-product-compliance
Lightning Source LLC
Chambersburg PA
CBHW011437170626
46808CB00009B/3082